Lock Down Publications and Ca$h Presents

HIDEOUS 2

A Bloody Nightmare

Written By

TOMMY COOK

First Edition 2026

Printed in the United States of America

Lock Down Publications
P.O. Box 944
Stockbridge, GA 30281
www.lockdownpublications.com

Like our page on Facebook: Lock Down Publications
www.facebook.com/lockdownpublications.ldp

Stay Connected with Us!

Text **LOCKDOWN** to 22828 to stay up-to-date with new releases, sneak peaks, contests and more…

Like our page on Facebook:
Lock Down Publications

Join Lock Down Publications/The New Era Reading Group

Visit our website:
www.lockdownpublications.com

Follow us on Instagram:
Lock Down Publications

Email Us: We want to hear from you!

Chapter 1

Beginning of a Nightmare

It's been almost two weeks since the death of Hideous' sister. He still couldn't believe she was gone. Shot right in front of him. It felt unreal, like a bloody nightmare. The bloodshed was just the beginning. He vowed on her dead soul he would find and kill Uzi Mi.

He had been hearing in the streets that Uzi Mi had fled to Miami. He was gon' pay him a visit with drums attached to AKs and ARs, but first he had to visit his T-Jones in the hospital. It been a while since he'd seen her.

He stepped inside the air-conditioned hospital and made his way toward the bank of elevators. He rode up to the fourth floor, where the ICU patients were kept. He continued down the long hallway to the room at the end. When he stepped inside, his heart didn't mourn for the bitch lying in the hospital bed, still healing from her wounds. She had a fractured jaw and broken ribs.

The only one person that ever loved him was dead. He sat next to his T-Jones' bed and watched her sleep peacefully—something he never experienced growing up.

"I hate you, bitch. You brought me and my twin more pain than anyone on earth. You might as well have been the one that pulled the trigger on Rachel. You probably were the one who tried to burn us years ago. I don't put shit past you. Fuck you. I hope yo' ass never wake up."

With that he stood to his feet and made his exit. Never looking back.

Jochebed opened her eyes once her son left, and a tear fell down her once-pretty face. She knew what he said was true. She was the one who tried to kill her own kids years ago. Truth be told, she hated them, but over time she learned to love them. As she closed her eyes, she drifted back to a time when she didn't have any kids and lived with no rules.

The atmosphere in *Exposure* was young and sexy, and she was the sexiest woman in the spot. Her two-piece thong and bra set showed all of her sexy curves, from her eye-catching figure to her bouncing ass that turned heads.

The Strella Kat look-alike was the shit everywhere she went. She was thick, with a small waist and a big ass that made heads spin. It even caught the attention of a killer. His eyes popped outta his head when he saw her thickness. He reached out and stopped her.

"Damn, ma, give a nigga a lap dance," he said, pulling out a dictionary size stack of cash.

Jochebed looked him up and down; he wasn't all that in the face, but his money would certainly do. She straddled his lap, pressing her titties against his chest. She wrapped her arms around his neck and grinded that pussy on his lap. "So, what's yo' name?" she whispered in his ear, making that ass bounce in his lap nonstop.

"Jephthah! I know you heard of me," he said, gripping her ass.

"Oh, shit," Jephthah uttered softly as he touched her big ol' titties.

Jochebed giggled, pretending she didn't hear the last shit he said. He was right, though—everybody in the streets that was getting it knew who he was. They better, or they were going to find themselves in a coffin, closed casket, with a burnt corpse inside.

Jephthah was the kind of nightmare the streets feared. A jack boy first, but a killer above all. He had the whole city shook. He knew his days were numbered. But he didn't give a fuck—before he left this world, the whole city was gon' bow down to his gangsta.

"You gon' be my babymama one day," he said.

"What?"

"My baby mama," he repeated. "No bullshit."

"Boy, please. I better not lose my figure giving birth to a muthafucka's seed."

"Yeah, we gon' see, ma! But make that ass clap for a real one."

She turned around, sat on his lap, and grinded her big ass in his crotch, making his dick hard as a rock. She had his undivided attention, so she bent over, grabbed his ankles, and put that big ass in his face, making her ass cheeks clap hard together like a church choir. When the song ended, she walked away, twerking her way across the club, disappearing into the crowd. She had him wanting more.

She headed to the empty locker room to change. She took off her bra and panties, tossing them into her bag. She was about to get sexy in a lil' maid outfit she'd picked up recently. When she looked up, she saw that ugly nigga with the money Jephthah behind her.

"What the fuck you doing in here, nigga?"

He looked at her pussy and said, "You didn't give me your number."

As time went by, everything fell into place for them. Jephthah showered her wit' expensive shit—money, cars, houses—and, most importantly, love. She was feeling herself, living the good life, ignoring all the warning signs. She had fallen deeply in love with a killer. His gangsta ass had her wanting to scream. She went from shaking her ass in *Exposure* for broke niggas to dining in five-star restaurants. But then, one day, everything changed drastically, like the weather shifting from summer to winter. His true colors began to show, and it was worse than she could have ever imagined.

When she walked into their two hundred-thousand-dollar crib that was bigger than a department store, she dropped her designer bags on the marble floor. The sounds that greeted her were unmistakable—the sounds of a woman moaning; she saw the pussy and ass getting drilled by her nigga.

"Ooooooh shit. Shit," came the sounds as soon as she entered. On the red-colored soft rug, Jephthah had a big-booty white bitch bent over. The bitch favored the white girl from the television show **Star**. Jephthah was pulling her hair and smacking her big white ass. He was fucking her hard. He never stopped pounding into her tight pink pussy. He made eye contact with Jochebed as he continued to pound mercilessly in the fat-booty white bitch.

"Who pussy dis is?" he asked the big-booty white bitch while staring his bitch in her eyes.

"Oh, my gawd. Yours. Yours," she screamed, looking into Jochebed's eyes with a smirk on her face. Jochebed knew exactly who the white girl was. They worked at the club together back in the day.

"You wrong as hell," was the only thing she could manage to say before the tears came rushing down her pretty face. She turned and left the room, never looking back.

A couple of hours later, when she returned home, she found him with yet another bitch—this time, a big-booty Mexican. They were in their bed fucking like two dawgs in heat. The Mexican bitch was riding her man's dick like she invented the position. Yet again, Jochebed's heart was torn apart and stomped on.

She made her way to leave again, but this time, before she reached the front door, Jephthah stopped her. He was butt ass naked, dick hard as hell with another bitch's juices on it, swinging in the air like a baby bat.

"Where you think you going?" he asked, hate burning in his eyes.

"I got to get away from you. How can you be so fucked up?" she said, but he covered her mouth with a kiss—only for that kiss to end fast with a punch she never saw coming. She crashed to the floor, tears blinding her vision, with mixed emotions and the taste of her own blood.

"What the fuck is wrong with you?" she screamed at him.

Wham. Wham. Wham.

He punched her over and over until she got the message. She was his bitch, and she wasn't going nowhere. "You think you can go out and shit on my name, huh, bitch? I love you. You think I don't love you, huh?" *Wham. Wham. Wham.*

The beating continued for what felt like an hour. "These bitches don't mean shit to me, bitch! I love you!" Jephthah stormed out the room, only to come back a moment later with the big-booty Mexican bitch. The girl was scared shitless. Jephthah had a Glizzy in his hand. He pressed it to the side of her head.

"You think I love this bitch, don't ya? This bitch doesn't mean shit to me, baby. You, my world. I love you!" He placed the barrel of the gun to the Mexican girl's forehead and blew her pretty face off. Her thoughts and memories of them erupted out the back of her skull. Her lifeless body dropped onto the marble floor. Blood poured down from her opened wound like hot oatmeal.

"Fuck dis bitch, baby!" Jephthah spat, shooting more slugs into the bitch's flesh. *Boc-Boc-Boc*.

Jochebed stared wide-eyed in terror, as he continued to pump the dead Mexican bitch wit' bullet holes. The only thing that ran through her mind was: *What the hell have I got myself into? I fell in love with a monster.*

Over the last couple of weeks, shit didn't get any better for Jochebed; they only got worse; she found herself rocking a black eye more often than makeup. She looked in the mirror and cried. The scar under her left eye reminded her of just how dangerous Jephthah was. The beatings grew worse and worse. She now hated her life. The fucked-up part was, after every beating her, he would fuck her even harder. She knew he was shooting his seed deep off in her womb to get her pregnant. That was something she didn't want—having a baby by a monster, or anybody else.

She turned to the side to examine her full figure; her ass was the fattest thing on her body. She had 46 inches of it, and some big, juicy ass titties. Her body put you in the mind of Dallas rapper Erica Banks.

When she stepped back into the master bedroom, Jephthah was sitting on the bed next to a mixed breed bitch that stripped at DG's. The bitch was bad with a figure that looked too perfect to be natural, something Jochebed knew was paid for.She had an ass like Bunz 4eva.

They both were naked. It was obvious they just got done fucking like two porn stars. She'd got over the fact that he showed her no respect whatsoever. Sometimes he made her participate in things she didn't want to. He made her do things her body hated. She tried to ignore their conversation, but how could she when the loud woman, talking like she was in her face, was saying enough for her to hear?

"I'm serious, bae, this laundromat is doing numbers."

"And how the fuck you know that?"

"I worked there, counting the money in the back. I'm going in tonight. Tonight will be the perfect time—ain't nun but two muthafuckas back there with me and another girl. But I got that handle already. Me and my bitch gon' distract them good." She patted her coochie like she would a good dog.

"I will look into it. Until then, let me make some calls," Jephthah said, standing and walking out of the room with his iPhone glued to his ear.

Chinky Eyz looked over at Jochebed and said, "Bitch, yo' man got some good ass dick," smiling as she knew it was getting under the pretty bitch's skin. Jochebed smiled and threw up her fuck-you finger before turning around to leave.

Later that night…

Jochebed sat on the bed, completely speechless as she watched her man and two of his minions, JB and Kenny, gear up in jack boy attire. She knew greed and power would eventually be his death, and she couldn't wait. She just watched as Chinky Eyz stood before them in a too-short Prada dress that covered nothing. Ass and pussy were on full display. She saw Jochebed looking, so Chinky Eyz bent over and started making her ass clap.

"Look, baby, I'm goin' to handle my part. All you got to do is yours. Come in hard, and let's get this money," she said, kissing Jephthah on the lips.

"How much we are looking at?" JB asked. He was a short, stocky muthafucka with a lot of tattoos all over his body. He was one of Jephthah's most loyal partnas since the sandbox.

"Nigga, that don't matter. What matters is getting it all," Jephthah spat. He watched as Chinky Eyz's ass jiggled as she walked out the front door. It was time to get some money, and he didn't love anything more than he did his back ends. JB and Kenny followed close behind him as he stepped out into the cool night breeze. Under his shirt, he was loaded with an Uzis. It was about to be a long night.

Chapter 2

Woo's Laundromat

When Chinky Eyz walked into the notorious laundromat known for moving tons of dope, everything looked the part. People were washing their clothes, kids were playing video games, and parents waited patiently for their clothes to be done.

But when she stepped inside the backroom that was locked with several heavy-duty locks, it felt like stepping onto a different planet. Two large tables sat in the middle with large stacks of money on top. There were copiers, rolls of plastic, tape, cardboard cartons, and a monitor displaying a quadrant of security cameras, mostly inside and outside of the laundromat, especially focused on the back door.

Two other half-naked bitches were counting stacks of dead presidents. One girl was a loudmouth Latina by the name of Spicy J. She wore loose-fitting shorts that showed off her tightly muscled, medium-tanned legs and well-rounded ass, with no bra. Her large tits sat high and proud on her fine chest, fully on display. The other bitch was a white girl that Chinky Eyz was cool with. She only met Spicy J twice before and was surprised to see her there tonight. Becky was naked from the waist down, except only for her heels. Her blouse was wide open, and her 38D tits hung out. As expected, two big Chinese steppers dressed in expensive Taylor made suits were watching their every move.

"Wassup, baby," Chinky Eyz said, running over to one of the steppers name Mink. "You kno' you miss me." She grabbed his dick and massaged it through his designer slacks.

"Hey, Chink," Mink said. He smiled and gestured for her to get naked. No clothes were permitted in the money room. Once she was fully naked, she walked over and stood next to her good friend, Becky. She was an ex-stripper herself that got turnt onto the game at the laundromat and was glad she did. She made a lot of money doing nothing.

"Don't worry about Spicy J; she about to leave," Becky informed her.

Chinky Eyz leaned over and said, "Let's have some fun, bitch. I'm not worrying about her. We 'bout to get paid." She began to run her fingers up and down Becky's wet slit as she looked over her shoulder at Mink and winked.

"God, Chinky, wait until she leaves," Becky panted.

"She can stay and watch. I like an audience." She looked over at the other Chinese man. His name was Le Pistols. He was six feet tall and very muscular, with brown hair and eyes and a deep baritone voice that would make any woman quake with excitement. He had a dragon tattoo on the side of his head. He watched as both bitches got freaky right there. Spicy J didn't know anything about the lick, but that's how Chinky Eyz wanted it. She made her way over to Le Pistols; he was seated in front of the large monitor watching everything that went on in his boss's shop.

He watched as they approached him. So did Spicy J. Chinky Eyz began running her right hand through his black hair, knowing he wanted her. She let her left hand unfasten his designer belt. He watched in lust as she slowly unzipped his pants. She got down between his legs and pulled them hoes down, right along with his boxers. He diverted his eyes from the monitor for a moment as Mink fucked Becky wit' long deep strokes. He turned his attention back to Chinky Eyz. She swallowed his entire shaft down her throat. A devious smirk formed on his lips. Lust flared in his eyes. There was an animalistic hunger in them.

She stroked his tiny dick in her hand, kissing it all around the head and slapping it on her wet tongue. Then, in on smooth motion, she swallowed his dick deep into her mouth. She damn neared swallow his balls with it. He couldn't take what headhunter skills. He grunted and came hard, his nut filling her mouth. She looked up at him and swallowed what remained in her mouth, then took his dick back in her mouth just to suck it clean.

With one hand, he grabbed her by the throat. With the other hand, he slapped up her titties. The sting shot through her body. He cupped her pussy and turned her around. Wit' her back to him and his to the monitor, he stuffed his dick in her violently. She began to slowly grind on the dick, up and down, back and forth. He bit down on her neck while Spicy J watched. She was lost for words. He yanked her by the hair and wedged his knee against her thigh, and forced her legs open wider. She glanced over her shoulder, watching him dig in her shit, but really, she was watching the monitor.

Becky, on the other hand, was getting fucked hard. Mink didn't give a fuck about Spicy J watching. He had Becky bent over the table, going ham, slamming his entire body into her like a head on collision.

"Oooooh shit!" she screamed out.

Outside…

Jephthah got out the whip and moved towards the front of the laundromat. He adjusted the ski mask on his face, then the Kevlar vest that read "FBI" printed on the front in bold yellow letters. His hit squad were right behind him, ready to get their hands bloody.

He put a finger to his lips as he opened the door and stepped inside. Kenny and Fox stepped in front, putting four muthafuckas on the floor. They sniffed the floor like an anteater.

"Shhh!" Fox whispered as he put a Mexican family of three down. "Were not going to hurt y'all. We only came for the cake."

Jephthah found the money room that had the **'Stop, you're not allowed'** sign posted. He led the way as the blast of gunfire shattered the door to the money room, showering plaster and brass down on him and the others in his crew.

The three of them flattened themselves against the wall. Jephthah was the first to speak. "Bitch, get on the ground! Drop your weapons! This is the FBI!" He knew there were two naked bitches in there, also counting money—one of them was his bitch, Chinky Eyz.

Right Before The Blast…

"Hold the hell up!" Le Pistols shouted, but Chinky Eyz kept slamming that big ass down on his dick. She looked over her shoulder and said, "You like this pussy, right? Your 'bout to bust, right?" The whole time she faked-moaned, staring right at the monitor at Jephthah, who was about to shoot the lock off. She hopped off the dick just as Le Pistols was shooting his nut in the air. She quickly grabbed the shotgun that sat on the table and knocked Le Pistols to the ground. She quickly aimed the sawed-off shotgun at Mink, who rocked a confused look.

"Baby, I got it under control in here as you can see," she yelled at Jephthah, but he ignored her and threw a smoke bomb into the room and heard a loud bang. The canister released a mist that dropped her and everybody else to the floor, hands over their watering eyes, coughing helplessly. "What the fuck is you doing? I said I got everything under control," Chinky Eyz yelled.

Jephthah fired a hail of hollow tips from the drake, knocking chunks off niggas and hoes. He stepped inside as bodies tumbled down like Legos. Fox and Kenny laughed as they stepped over the dead that were scattered on the ground.

Jephthah looked around the laundromat. Just as Chinky Eyz had described it, money was scattered all over the table and stacked up in a corner of the room. There was a safe also; five by three by two, and it was open, saving him the trouble of blowing into the door with explosive charges.

The safe was full of kilos of heroin and more stacks of money. Jephthah picked up one of the kilos and examined the Chinese letter stamped on the front. He didn't have a slight idea what the symbol meant.

"Dawg, what the fuck is that shit?" Fox asked.

"It doesn't matter. Pack the shit and let's go." Jephthah shot back, staring at Chinky Eyz dead body riddled with bullets holes. *You thought you was gon' come up off my get down. Bitch, you had me fucked up*, he thought, smirking.

As all three of them packed the money and drugs, they heard a racking cough coming from one the bitches on the floor. Jephthah found her lying on her side. It was Spicy J; she was all messed up but still breathing. She looked up. Her face was swollen from the pepper bomb. He aimed the Drake and flipped her insides out like gymnastics.

"Boss, look out," Kenny called out. He pointed at something in the back of the safe that he missed. There were at least ten small packets of synthetic K2. With the duffle bags of cash and dope already packed, it was time to go. The three of them made several trips in and out of the laundromat, taking it all.

The riches were enormous—$389 racks in cash, 21 bricks of fentanyl, and 10 packets of K2.

Back At Jephthah's Crib…

JB and his little brother Kenny were counting the munyun as Jephthah stood a few feet away. Jochebed was in the kitchen making, dinner for the man she hated with all her guts. The house was loud with Montana 700's new song blasting in the background.

Jephthah stood there with a Glock in his hand. Jochebed kept looking over her shoulder, sensing something wasn't right. Her man was fidgeting too much. Just when she started adding seasoning to the rice, she heard a familiar sound.

Fa—Fa—Fa—Fa—Fa.

She watched the shot rip through Kenny's face, ripping a chunk of flesh from the side of his neck, blood gushing from the wound. JB reacted quickly, springing into action, but not quick enough. Jephthah pulled the trigger, blowing a hole through the right side of his head. His brain leaked out over his shoulder, looking like shredded cabbage.

Jochebed ran over once his body hit the ground. Kenny's body was still twitching. Jephthah filled him up with more bullets. She couldn't believe the monster she had been lying next to every night. He reached down and picked up the bloody money.

"Clean this shit off," he demanded, making his way to the back with a lot of blood on him.

***

Somewhere In China…

Suwoo Chan glanced down at his gold presidential Rolex and saw the time was too damn late to be getting a damn call from one of his top lieutenants in America.

"Do you not see the time, Dragon?"

"It's urgent, sir, and I do apologize."

He looked over to his left at his lovely wife and rubbed her naked ass. She looked just like IG model **@justblahgigi**. Even though he was Chinese, he loved his sistas, especially the thick ones. He looked over to his other side at his other wife, who was pregnant with his baby. He rubbed her ass also. He rose from his current position and easily got out the bed. He walked out his million-dollar-plus penthouse and leaned over the rail.

"What the fuck can be so urgent? I'm with my wives, and one is pregnant with my baby."

"Some niggers ran inside one of your laundromats tonight in Dallas. The thieves got away with $380,000 thousand, sir, some kilos."

"How many?" Suwoo Chan was beyond stunned.

"Twenty-one.

"Say no more. I'm on my way!" With that, he disconnected the call, already knowing he had to fly out to Dallas. Who had enough balls to try him? He didn't know, but he wanted to meet and kill them.

Chapter 3

Jealousy

A Couple of Days After the Robbery…

Jephthah's jaw twitched, and he tightened his hand into a fist, squeezing his rage. He watched as Jochebed gave a nasty lap dance to a light-skinned nigga with VVS diamonds in his mouth, lighting up like the Fourth of July every time he opened them.

She had no idea Jephthah was there creeping into the night. The nigga handed her his iPhone, and she locked her number into it before getting up and walking off. Her ass was doing back flips, flipping every which way, moving smoothly like water.

On her way back towards the bar, she locked eyes with him. She dropped her head to her chest. Tears welled up in her eyes. She knew the outcome later would be a bloody lip and a busted nose. When she lifted her head back up, she exhaled slowly and walked towards Jephthah in nothing but a money-green G-string.

He had his back flat against the wall, smoking a potent blunt. He blew smoke into the air as his eyes burned a hole in the back of the light-skinned nigga's head.

"Who dat pussy ass nigga was?" The first thing he said when she made her way in front of him.

"A nobody. He's not even from the city. He's from Orange, Texas," she said quickly in her defense, like she was up against a top D.A.

His jaw twitched some more. He grabbed her by her panties and pulled her to him. "Since you want to *he-he* and *ha-ha* with the nigga. You gon' put me in his pockets."

"And how am I supposed to do that?"

Jephthah dipped his finger in her pussy. "With this fat muthafucka." She put a hand on his shoulder when he got to going deeper and deeper inside her lil' pussy. "Now get yo' ass back over there and make this shit happen for the both of us."

They both looked over at the light-skinned nigga that said his name was BayBay. He was thugging with his niggas now, having a good time, not knowing he was probably going to die tonight. Jealousy was an evil man's poison, and the way Jephthah was looking at BayBay made Jochebed's heart shiver. She couldn't lie. She could see why he was jealous; unlike Jephthah's ugly ass, BayBay was extremely handsome. He made her heart melt. He was short, around her height, with long dreads. His jewelry told another story. It lit the room. And his pockets were on big boy status. You could see the ice in his mouth from a mile away.

I bet his lil short ass got a fat ass dick, she thought, at the wrong time. She could actually feel the heat coming from her man's body.

She made her way back over to BayBay. Her fat ass booty was bouncing like a basketball and jiggling like a maintenance man's keys. She gave him a good look at her camel toe as she eased back in front of her.

"Who dat nigga looking all over here on top of yo' head?" he asked.

"Some trick trying to pay for some ass."

"He just doesn't know you coming back to Orange with me."

"What makes you think dat?"

"You came back to me, didn't you?"

"I did, but do I look easy to you? And what makes you think I'm going all the way to Orange with a nigga I don't know?"

"You came back to me, didn't you?" he said again.

"I did, but do I look easy to you?"

"Definitely not. Come sit with me though. Let's catch up. I'm trying to take you back with me. I need to see you pop dat ass on me again though. That shit fat as fuck."

She turned the opposite way to display her fat ass to him. She spread her legs wide, bent over with all pussy showing from the back. She put her hands on her knees and made her ass do a fool like her name was Sukihana. The entire time her ass clapped for strangers, she made eye contact with a man that had already killed three muthafuckas in front of her. The look in his eyes told her he was about to claim another body before the night was over. But that night, BayBay got away. He wasn't a fool. No bitch could play on his top.

Later That Night...

Jochebed was on the bed on all fours with her juicy ass cocked up in the air. Jephthah had her by the hips, killing her pussy, on the verge to busting inside her.

"Please, don't nut in me. I don't want to get pregnant!" She knew her words went in one ear and out the other, because every time they fucked, he nutted deep inside of her.

She didn't want to have a baby by no nigga, especially not by him. She was afraid a baby would ruin her perfect shape and make her fat and slow—something she didn't want. But Jephthah saw it another way to get her to bow down to him, and only him.

He longed-dicked in and out of her lil' wet pussy, real slow, watching the effects of her juicy ass as it bounced off his dick. He leaned down and spat between her ass cheek, then used his thumb to rub it around her hole.

For a long minute, he fucked her hard from the back, then suddenly he pulled out. He went to the foot of the bed and motioned for her. She slid her sexy ass toward him and her legs straight up into the air. He wrapped a hand around each of her ankles as he guided his long dick into her wet ass pussy.

He fucked her with long deep strokes that made her eyes water up and rolled to the back of her head. Her juicy titties bounced all over her chest.

"Damn, this dick good, nigga!" she screamed, shaking her head from side to side. She probably hated his guts, but she loved the dick. He continued to fuck her all night.

2 Weeks Later…

Jephthah swung his body out the red Tesla Model S, which had parked near the curb. He had stalked BayBay for two long weeks. He done robbed niggas in Dallas, Fort Worth, Houston, and finally, *The Golden Triangle*. Tonight, he was going to rob one of the main niggas getting it out that way. And he was going to kill him, execution-style.

Baybay made the mistake of his life when he came to Dallas to throw money like he done robbed an armored truck—which he had, a week before.

And now, less than thirty yards away across the street, there was BayBay himself. Jephthah watched the big money nigga climb out of a sleek, blue candy-painted 2025 Lexus RX. He wore a white wife beater, royal blue designer jeans, and Jays to match. His bust-down Cuban link looked like a streetlight, dancing in the night air.

A big-booty high-yellow bitch that looked like some off *Baddies* was with him. She wore a short Burberry dress, looking good enough to eat. She was laughing at something he said, throwing her head back. Even though the bitch was acting just to lure him in, Jephthah still felt some type of way by how his bitch fed into his ego. If it wasn't for her, BayBay would've kept his riches and his life.

BayBay carried a small black duffel bag full of $44 racks and three birds he got from his connect. Jephthah watched as they both disappeared into his two-story house. When he reached the door, he was fully charged. The highly polished mahogany double doors opened right in his face. He stared at Jochebed's thick naked frame. She was completely naked, except for the diamond necklace.

Could it be that easy? Robbing a high-level drug trafficker like BayBay? The nigga didn't have no cameras or shooters; he was just wide open for anybody to touch.

Jochebed was scared, visibly tense. "He's in the back. He thinks I'm getting something to drink. Can we please make this as quick as possible?" She clearly didn't want any part of Jephthah's murderous plot. She knew he was a monster. He'd played her into doing this stupid shit. It was her first and last time. She had to admit, though, BayBay was extremely easy to control. She knew he wasn't used to anything that looked as good as her. So, it was easy for her to entice him, especially with how she moved her fat ass and bounced them big titties in his face. He wanted her around to show off like a championship ring.

"He's drunk, completely fucked up," she whispered as they stood in the dark foyer of the enormous house. She could see the sawed-off shotgun Jephthah carried by his side. She turned on her bare heels, and he followed her. He watched her juicy ass jiggle as they walked through the enormous living room, dimly lit by a hallway lamp. This was the way to the master bedroom.

An AK stood proudly beside the stone fireplace. The sight of the high-powered assault rifle turned Jephthah up. He was ready to taste blood. They walked into the bedroom together.

"I'm back, baby. Did you miss me?" Jochebed asked.

"Fuck yeah," BayBay answered quickly.

"Surprise, bitch nigga!" Jephthah announced, aiming the sawed-off shotgun at his face. BayBay bolted up in his bed, surprised and angry at the same time.

"What the fuck? What the . . . who the fuck are you? How the fuck you get in here?" His words were slurred, making it impossible to understand.

Jephthah opened the Goyard bag and handed it to Jochebed.

"Bitch, you're in on this?" BayBay gasped as he looked around at the thick yellow bitch. She put her head down. The grief ate her up from the inside. When she looked up, Jephthah had the shotgun pressed to BayBay's forehead.

"Please, you don't got to do this. I got seven kilos of coke under my bed in a Louis V bag." He was sober now. His thoughts were coming in clear now. He had a fucking shotgun sitting on his temple. He was that nigga in his city. He touched $100 racks and had motion. He could've bought any shooter around his way. Now he was caught with his pants down.

Jephthah pulled the trigger without any remorse. BayBay's head exploded like a chunk of ice being thrown hard on the concrete. The shot shattered the back of his skull leaving his shit looking like an open garage door.

"Oh, my gawd!" Jochebed screamed before throwing up whatever she ate that day.

"Bitch, help me with this shit," Jephthah shouted, stuffing the seven bricks in a pillow cases. "Do you hear, bitch?"

She nodded. Her face was growing pale. She looked weak. Still, she took a long, deep breath and helped her man. She grabbed the bag with the money and three bricks. After they had everything, they left as quickly as they came in.

Chapter 4

Nine Months Later

Inside the enormous trap house in North Dallas, Jochebed sat on a cream leather sofa, her stomach as big as a wagon. She was done crying her soul out. Her worst fear had come true—she was nine months pregnant with not one baby, but two. She was having twins by a monster. If he had died at any point during her pregnancy, she would've gotten an abortion, but every day he came back walking through the door with bloody clothes and bloody money. He was a nightmare to the streets. Niggas feared him even more now than when he had nothing but a wish and a gun.

But his torments on the streets finally caught up with him. He'd crossed the wrong muthafuckas. Some crazy-ass Chinese muthafuckas were out trying to claim his soul. Nine months ago, he robbed the wrong laundromat, one that belonged to an underground crime syndicate led by Suwoo Chan. He was the feared leader of the *Red Dragon Triads*. The only thing they wanted now was his life.

After Suwoo Chan stepped foot on American soil, he searched for the muthafuckas who had balls like lions. He searched every hood and came up empty-handed. After six months, he finally put $100K on the muthafuckas who stole from him like he wasn't the most feared man in China. But Jochebed wouldn't find out about that until three months later.

"Bitch, you still ain't dressed?" Jephthah said as he stepped into the living room, two bad bitches in tow, ones he had selling pussy and stripping. He just didn't know he was walking straight into a trap laid by the bitch he loved. Unbeknownst to him, Jochebed had called and set it up to deliver him straight to the devil himself. She couldn't wait to get to Dallas Cabaret.

The thing was, over time, Jephthah had grown a following of nothing but YNs. They were at least forty deep, and they loved the money they made with their boss. They were nothing at first—just a bunch of bums the streets threw out like trash. Jephthah was their savior.

"Nigga, kill dat shit. Why yo' hoes ain't dressed?"

"Hoes!" Fatty Bobo snapped her neck to the side and shifted her weight to the left. She was a thick redbone with sandy red hair and freckles. She stood at 4'11" with enough ass to feed an island. She rocked a tiny black Gucci dress with nothing underneath. She kept having to pull the dress down over her fat ass.

"Naw, bitch, you the hoe. Don't think a bitch won't get on your ass because you pregnant," Robin spat. She was also a bad bitch. She was thick, like Instagram model Thicky Minaj. She rocked blonde hair with tattoos all over her sexy ass body, mainly on her hefty ass.

"Chill, the bitch pregnant with my seeds," Jephthah said in a serious tone, and both bitches put their heads down.

"You better get them hoes. I swear to gawd," Jochebed snapped, her eyes narrowing as they glared at Jephthah, her hand resting on her pregnant belly.

"Bitch, hold yo' tongue and get dressed. My niggas should be pulling up."

On The Other Side of Town…

Under a beautiful Dallas Sky, a dozen *shashou*—which simply means "killer" in Chinese—stood fully dressed in

Gucci and Prada suits. They were lined up in front of luxury vehicles from Lambos to Rarris, even a Bugatti was present. The *shashous* stood among a powerful man, Suwoo Chan. He was a gangster.

The two bad bitches that stood on each side of him held all *his shashou's* attention. He spoke with power in his tone, and each word sounded like thunder.

“Each of you are here for one sole purpose,” Suwoo Chan said. “And that is to kill the nigga that stole from me! I want his head and both of his hands.”

Dallas Cabaret…

When Jephthah and Jochebed pulled up to the club, it was as if the president and the first lady had just arrived. All eyes were on them as the most feared man in the city pulled up in a red Hellcat.

He stepped out Jochebed on his arm. Behind them were his entourage and two bad bitches. His entourage rocked all black, with enough ice to start their own jewelry store. They walked into the club and went straight to VIP, where it was supposed to be reserved for only them. But to Jephthah's surprise, a bunch of well-dressed Chinese men had it on lock. They were popping bands and bottles.

Jephthah and his entourage made their way over and stepped behind the red velvet rope. He pulled aside one of the bottle girls, who was half-naked.

"Why the fuck are them muthafuckas invading my space? I paid for the whole session."

"You did, but they came with a price the club's owner couldn't refuse. Now, do you want it? If not, we can move you to a table or a booth and give you your money back."

“I'm good. I'm not ‘bout to let no shrimp-fried-rice-eating muthafuckas run me outta my session,” he shot back and took his seat next to his bitch. He looked over at the Chinese thugs. They had nearly all the strippers popping ass and shaking big ol' titties.

There was one thug Jephthah noticed wasn't doing shit but staring his way with a hard look on his face. His name was Dragon. He was Suwoo Chan's top hitman. He sat between two thick strippers until one got up, rocking a big-ass booty. She walked over to the bar with two Chinese thugs behind her. Whoever she was, she was deeply rooted.

At that moment, the other stripper got up and walked to the ladies' room. That was weird to Jephthah.

"What's wrong, bae?" Jochebed asked.

"Something don't feel right," he said as he surveyed the club with a wary eye.

"I know it doesn't. But you know why I did it?" She leaned over to whisper in his ear. "I hate your ass so much. These Chinese killers 'bout to fuck you up. Remember that laundromat you robbed? It belonged to them." She got up and walked away, disappearing into the crowd.

By the time Jephthah pieced the puzzle together, it hit him like breaking news. The only person who could betray him was the one person he trusted with his life. He looked for her, and what he saw tore him apart on the inside. She was walking out of the club.

He cut his eyes at Dragon. He smiled in Jephthah's direction. One of the strippers sat in Dragon's lap with a Draco in her hand, aiming it in Jephthah's direction. She didn't fire until fifteen masked men gun appeared out of nowhere. It was like something straight out of a movie scene. They began firing handguns and assault rifles. More than 50 rounds were fired.

Budda-Budda—

The sound of the shots echoed through the club as Jephthah ducked behind one of his men, narrowly avoiding the barrage of bullets.Not long after the shots, Dallas Cabaret turned into a blood bath. Bodies dropped, but not the right body. Jephthah tried to run, shoving muthafuckas out of his way. He managed to make it near the front door with a handful of YNs still trying to play hero. But Dragon's men were knocking shit back. Fifteen guns were cutting shit down.

Jephthah ran outside the club, leaving his men behind to deal with his mess. When he made it into the night breeze, his eyes lit up like a Christmas tree. A handful of *shashous* stood in front of him. They each had a military-grade weapon in their hands. They let him have it. His body moved like Denzel's on *Training Day*, all around like a wet noodle.

Much Later…

Jochebed exited the Escalade with two Chinese *shashous*. They walked into the back of a hookah bar in Deep Ellum. Four Chinese men stood on each side of the door, toting some real heavy heat. She noticed a Chinese man sitting alone at a table full of money. He was playing chess by himself. He looked like a thug. His rough complexion suggested a childhood of hard living. His narrow eyes emitted a cold glare—he looked like a man you'd want on the opposite side of a gun.

Suwoo Chan looked at Jochebed. "A simple question. Who was that man I killed tonight to you?"

"The father of my unborn babies," she said quickly. There was a long pause. She was lost in a sea of white light from the lamp on the table, waiting for the man with so much power to say anything. He gave her a permanent chill, a simmering fear that escalated to a full boil whenever she let her imagination wander to thoughts of dying.

He leaned in, a gleam in his eye. "Why did you give me the man who carries your babies that way?"

"I'm glad he's dead."

"Then why share your body with a man like that and have his baby?"

"You mean *babies*. I'm having twins by a monster. I never wanted them. If he'd died earlier, they would've too."

"My wife's having a baby, too. She's probably due around the same time as you. I can't wait to meet the little guy."

At that moment, a white waitress with big-ass titties came by with a serving tray that contained alcoholic drinks and a line of coke. She walked away giggling after Suwoo Chan smacked her on the ass, the ripple spreading like a wave or some shit, moving like water.

"The man who carried your babies stole a lot of money from me. Do you know where it is?"

"No, he kept that shit away from the house."

Suwoo Chan was a hardened leader who had spent most of his life free. He was smart and had a way of looking through a muthafucka's soul, knowing when they were lying or telling the truth.

"Do you know that because of him, for the rest of your life, you'll be indebted to me?"

"I just want my money. Whatever he did isn't on me. I did what you asked. Now it's time to get paid. You look like a man of your word."

It was silent again in the room for a long time. Finally, the money arrived, and it was time for her to collect and go.

"I'll be seeing you soon," Suwoo Chan promised her.

As soon as the money was packed into a Goyard bag, she threw the bag over her shoulder. She was about to make her exit when her water broke.

Chapter 5

Dirty Diapers

One Year Later…

Jochebed hung up the phone and headed to the closet to retrieve some clothes. She looked over at her bed and noticed her one-year-old son, Reuben, staring at her. He never smiled or cried. He just watched everything with a mug.

"What the fuck yo' ugly ass looking at?" she screamed at him. He just sat there with his fat fist in his mouth, looking over at his twin sister, who was still asleep. Now, she was the crybaby that Jochebed couldn't stand.

After quickly putting on some boy shorts and a tank top, he decided to head to the kitchen. She got her baby boy a bottle and warmed that hoe up. When she made it back, she handed it to him, and he took it at once. She sat on the bed next to him, rubbing lotion all over her body. The $100 thousand dollars she had over a year ago had disappeared. Now, she was back shaking her juicy ass, which had gotten fatter after having her kids.

The only thing Jephthah's sorry ass left her was a run-down house in the Nawf and two shitty ass babies. Unbeknownst to her, he was living a secret life. He already had twins with a bitch he was married to in Miami, where he was born and raised. When he died, she got everything, leaving Jochebed with nothing but debt from a shitload of angry hustlers.

Later…

"Girl, make yourself at home," Jochebed told her best friend, Lisa Parker. Lisa was a bad bitch. She was built like Dallas rapper Bunz 4eva. She was *that* bitch anywhere she went. She was a solid five-five, with a pretty face and an ass so thick, it had Jochebed saying to herself, *"Damn. All that ass."*

"Bitch, why you didn't tell me that house down the street was for sale?" Lisa asked as she sat on the sofa with her oldest son, Shoota Face. He was a couple of years older than Jochebed's kids and bad as hell.

"Shid, I got so much shit going on, I didn't know. Do you know my sperm donor left me with all his bullshit, while that ugly-ass Cuban bitch he was married to is somewhere living her best life?"

"That was some fucked-up shit he did to you, leaving you behind like that after he done robbed most of the city. That couldn't had been me, no ma'am."

"I know, right? Look at him, he's getting big, girl." Jochebed picked Shoota Face up. "Where's Sarah?"

"Somewhere with her daddy. You know he love him some of her." Lisa looked around, looking for her godkids. "Where Rachel and Reuben?"

"Them bitches in the back, sleeping. Look, I might be late getting home tonight. I gotta make this money for this nigga named Fly. He says Jephthah owed him $17 racks. He keeps popping up over here, talking about what he gon' do if I don't pay him."

"Bitch, on some real shit, you can't keep putting your body through so much for a dead nigga that wasn't even treating you right."

"I know, right? Hopefully, he leaves me and my babies alone," she said, throwing on a short, tight dress. On a slow night, she made close to three grand. She knew she was about to fuck them up tonight. The whole city was gon' be out for the hood awards hosted at DG's.

Club DG's
12:10 p.m.

Jochebed's dress was halfway up her ass by the time she entered the club. A "bounce that ass" song was on, and hoes were already touching their knees and elbows. The bitch was packed more than any other night. She rubbed her hands together when she saw Bless, the club's manager. She tried to duck his ass, but he yanked her lil' ass up anyway and pulled her into his office.

"I know you not sellin' ass in my club and I'm not gettin' my cut, bitch," he said, venom in his tone. He pulled her dress all the way up her bare ass. She didn't rock no panties. She let out a long sigh and whispered, *"What are you doing?"*

"Shut the fuck up, bitch," he replied. He dug his fingers into her pussy, stroking them in and out, curling them up to graze her G-spot. "You know Jephthah owed me money, too." He pushed her down on her knees and pulled his designer jeans down just enough for her to pull his dick out. He slapped her in the face with it a couple of times. "Open your mouth."

She obeyed and took him deep in her mouth, sucking faster while tears threatened to fall freely down her face. She couldn't believe she was paying for Jephthah's sin.

He wasted no time pounding her hard and fast, forcing her to cum back-to-back all over his dick. He slammed into her with so much force that her entire ass wobbled with each stroke.

Bless busted a strong nut all over her back and ass and got rid of her like a bad habit. "If I find out you sellin' pussy and not giving me no munyun, I'm gon' beat yo ass."

They came out of the office together. She went one way, and he went the other. She kept pulling her dress down as she walked away in silence, her heart heavy. As she stood there, with her bow-legged stance, a pimp nigga by the name of Fly came up behind her, kissing the back of her neck and ear. She knew it was him—he was the only one that smelled like funky, cheap-ass cologne. He cupped and squeezed her soft, juicy ass aggressively.

"You got my money yet?" he asked, his hand slowly drifting under her ass and slipping between her legs, rubbing her naked pussy.

"Nigga, I literally just got here. Let me get out this dress first."

"You right, bitch, go on and get daddy his money." Fly smacked her ass, making it jiggle nonstop.

Jochebed looked around the club and saw it was filled to capacity. Hustlers of all types were in that bitch. You had your dope boys turning up on one side with their killers and workers bunched around them more than the bitches were. Then you had your jackboys watching them like hawks, ready for the liquor to control their minds and emotions. Then you had the worst of the worst—the broke niggas pretending to have some type of motion but really were in last place, trying to be something they weren't, rocking fake jewelry like it was real. She hated them. All they did was waste your time with empty promises and fake dreams.

She ditched the dress and came back out in nothing but a money-green G-string. She did what Bossman D-low said—*shake dat ass*. She held her bare tits as she walked through the crowd, making her ass jiggle like water in a balloon sloshing around. When she made it to the stage, she opened her mouth and stuck out her tongue like the freak bitch she was. Niggas stood around with lustful eyes, each of them throwing stacks in the air as her ass jumped higher like a rabbit or a frog.

Bills piled up on the stage, higher and higher.

After she finished her performance, she picked up all her money and strutted off toward the highest bidder. She left with a lanky, dark-skinned nigga with a bald head and diamonds in his mouth, shining hard like the sun. He was a hustler from Woodtown. His name was Courney Black. He had old money. He was in his late forties. She was twenty-one with a fat ass and a wet pussy. She looked back at it as it did backflips real fast and succulent in Courney Black's face.

It bounced like a kangaroo trying to save its ass.

"Damn, come back to the crib with me. My money's good. My nigga Fly said you good. You selling pussy off in this bitch," he said, hypnotized by her figure, which was 38DD-26-45.

Jochebed looked up and saw Fly standing near them, trying to ear-hustle. What choice did she have? *Come on, I got a spot.* She took him by the hand and led him to the men's restroom, where she was stopped by the nigga passing out gum and spraying niggas down with cheap cologne.

"Bitch, where's my fee?"

"I got you. Let me use one of the stalls."

"Hurry up, and I better get my cut."

Ten minutes later, she heard, "Mmgh. Grrr." He groaned into her ear as he stroked hard and mercilessly until he bust all in the condom he got from Mr. Cologne Man.

Jochebed was exhausted and walked over to where Fly sat, finishing his drink.

"You got my money?"

She nodded grimly. "I don't appreciate you telling these niggas I'm selling pussy for you like you my trick or some shit."

"You see that fat nigga over there?" He ignored her like a broke nigga would a begging bitch. He pointed west toward the main stage.

She nodded back even more grimly. She knew where he was going with this.

"Bring me back that bag."

"I'm not yo' hoe. You go fuck him!"

He grabbed her by the neck and roughed her up, grabbing her pussy and rubbing his thumb across her clit vigorously. She closed her eyes and threw her head back.

"Do you want me to fuck you up in this bitch?"

"Ummmm, no," she cried while he continued to misuse her body and mind.

"Well, get yo' bitch ass over there!"

A moment later, she walked into Big Devin's booth. He was sitting back like he was Rick Ross, the biggest boss. She knew what time it was, and so did he. He reached into his Amiri jeans, pulling out the biggest dick she had ever laid eyes on.

"You know what it is, hoe," he said, staring at every inch of her body. Her pussy was fat, damn near about to bust through her panties. She looked at his huge dick and couldn't believe what Fly wanted her to do. Even though Jephthah was dead, he still made her life pure hell. He owed damn near the whole city. Niggas that put him on licks—now, she was paying for it.

She wondered if his wife was going through the same shit in Miami. She doubted it. If anybody knew he was married, it wasn't her.

"Bring yo' sexy ass over here," Big Devin said, stroking the hell out of his dick. She did as she was told. She thought if she did what Fly wanted her to do, he would leave her the fuck alone. But $7,000 was a lot of money. She didn't have that much pussy to go around.

"What are you trying to do to me right here in front of everybody?" she hummed in his ear.

"Bitch, don't worry about shit. My niggas got us covered." At least three of his men were up, shielding them from wandering eyes. He pulled down her panties and turned her around into reverse cowgirl. Before long, lustful moans filled the air. He stabbed into her gushy pussy, making it sound like a washing machine as he jackhammered inside her. He fucked her so hard in a rhythm that the sofa banged against the wall. His fast and powerful strokes were too much for her. His balls slammed against her ass like a sledgehammer trying to go through drywall.

They fucked like they were the only ones in the club. Like they didn't care who heard. The smell of sex filled the air around them. He was the third nigga to have his dick in her that night alone. He went hard for the next twelve minutes until she felt his nut skeet inside of her.

"Oh . . . shit," he panted, pushing her off him. "Lil Dude, pay this bitch, and give her some extra to get a Plan B." All his niggas chuckled while he needed a few minutes to recoup.

Chapter 6

Becoming A Monsta

After Jochebed dressed and calmed down, she sat at her dressing room table and spread the money she had just made off Big Devin across the top. Not bad for one nigga. In the reflection of the mirror, she saw the hate in the other hoes' eyes. They were selling pussy too, but all the drug dealers wanted her. She rolled her eyes and put her money up in her locker.

As soon as she stepped back into the packed club, a bottle girl with a fat pussy named Mattie walked up on her and handed her a piece of paper. "From the nigga over there." She pointed at Fly. Jochebed rolled her eyes and opened the paper. He wanted her to fuck some local rapper that had just walked in the club. His name was Got Bandz. He was barely 18. And he wanted her to drop his money off. He was leaving.

She was fed up. She walked through the crowded club with one thing on her mind: murder. She never killed a muthafucka before, but she didn't have a choice. Fly was getting out of control. She wasn't a nigga's hoe. She had to get rid of the problem. She didn't fuck random niggas. She didn't fuck for money, and she damn sho' wasn't about to get pimped out for her dead ass sperm donor.

On her way out of the club, Bless stuck his head out of the office. "Bring yo' ass here. Where the fuck you think you going?"

"I got to get to my babies. The babysitter ain't gon' keep them all night."

"Bullshit, I seen when yo' pimp left, and I also seen when you handed him his money. Where mines?"

"Look, he ain't my pimp. I don't have time for this shit. I got to get my babies. Here, this is all I got. She handed him $300 dollars." She looked down at the Glock he had sitting in plain view. She guessed he put it there to scare her.

"Baby. Baby." A thick ass chocolate stripper came running inside the office. He looked up at the bitch with a serious expression written across his face. "They 'bout to fight, come quickly."

"Ugh, wait here, bitch, this shit not over between us. You owe me more than what you are giving." He followed the big-ass booty out the office.

He had her fucked up. She stole a peek behind her back and quickly grabbed the gun. She exited the office quickly as she came.

A couple of minutes later, she stepped outside and saw Fly and two of hoes smoking in the parking lot, sitting inside his red Range Rover with black limo tint. He sat there smoking and collecting. He looked up and saw his new favorite hoe. She walked towards his whip with the note he left for her in her hand.

Jochebed's eyes shifted from side to side as if she were wanted for murder.

"Go get my money," he barked at his two hoes. They both climbed out the back and walked back towards the club. Jochebed slid inside and scanned the area again.

"Bitch, where Got Bandz?"

"He said later. He was trying to turn up with his niggas," Jochebed lied. She didn't even see the nigga. She was too busy trying to leave and catch his ass.

"That's okay. I got a room close by and another trick waiting to get some pussy for one of my girls." Fly pulled out in traffic. Jochebed jumped when she felt his hand trying to ease its way up her small dress. In no time he was rubbing her pussy. She smiled while keeping her hand gripped on her new gun inside her purse.

They pulled into a run-down hotel off Harry Hines. If Fly he wasn't trying to be so nasty, he would've seen the gun now in her hand. But it was too late. She aimed and pulled the trigger, killing him instantly. That was the first time she ever killed somebody.

Present Day…

Not long after that night, Jochebed turned into a monster. She was killing everything that fucked over her. It was a dark secret she never wanted a soul to know. When Hideous started to get older, she could see the same hate in his heart his father once had in his. She knew he was going to be a problem to the streets, so it didn't surprise her when after the fire, he was accused of killing someone at the tender age of fourteen.

When she opened her eyes, wet tears fell down her once-pretty face. She couldn't believe the monster she had become. She remembered the night of the fire like it was yesterday. She was the one who started it. She sat up in the hospital bed and rubbed her eyes. She wiped away the tears because she knew more tears were coming.

***

Nine Years Ago…

Jochebed screamed as she watched the flames spread quickly. Her two young kids were inside. She could hear her ten-year-old daughter screaming, but really she didn't give two fucks about that bitch's tears.

Just before the fire—before neighbors crowded the street—she crept into the garage, grabbed a small red gasoline container, and poured it all over the house from the inside, starting with the living room and ending with her kids' room.

As Jochebed got back outside and watched her house burn, she began to scream.

Hideous' eyes snapped open, and he sat up in bed when he heard his T-Jones screaming. But as he listened closely, he realized it was his twin's voice. He rubbed his eyes and saw the flames as smoke engulfed the room.

"Rachel!"

He hopped out of bed and sprinted toward the flames. Any other ten-year-old would have been too scared to move, but the only person he loved needed him. She wasn't strong like him. It was like she had all his soft emotions, because he had none.

He ran through the flames that were spreading wildly. When he made it to his twin's bedroom, he tried to open the door, but the knob burned his hand.

He looked around and saw nothing he could use to pry it open.

Then he heard his T-Jones' voice.

"Somebody. Please, save my kids. Please," she screamed.

"Mama."

Hideous ran through the flames once more to the front door. Luckily for him, it wasn't as hot as his twin's doorknob. He opened the door and locked eyes with a bitch he had hated all his life.

He knew he had to save his own sister.

He quickly turned and rushed back into the burning house, running through the flames once more.

He knew he had to his sister.

"Reubeeennn," he heard his T-Jones scream, knowing she didn't give a fuck about him. She could've gotten an Oscar for her performance.

On his way towards his twin's room, he picked up a dish rag from the kitchen sink. It was already wet, so it saved him some time. He put the wet rag on the doorknob and opened it. He looked around and heard her muffled cries from underneath her bed. He quickly grabbed her tiny hand and the two of them ran through the flames.

An inch away from the front door the roof collapsed on top of Hideous. He had enough strength to stiff-arm his sister out of harm's way. "Go, save yourself," he yelled. But before Rachel could react, a hand grabbed her from behind. She looked up and saw her next-door neighbor Mr. Anthony pulling her out the burning house.

"No. My brother. Please help him."

"Sorry, chile, but there's nothing nobody can do for him." Mr. Anthony looked back at the blazing flames. Hideous managed to look up and saw his sister being pulled out to safety. They gave him enough strength to push whatever was on top of him off. He crawled underneath the debris.

"Look," a man from the crowd yelled, pointing at the front door of the blazing house.

"Rachel . . . Rachel." That was all he could manage to get out before everything around him went dark. The only sound he could hear was his T-Jones heart-rending screams.

Chapter 7

Wanted For Murder

Hideous was silent, trying to stem the rage that was building in up inside his heart. He should've killed the bitch when he had the chance. But instead, he drove away from the hospital with a lot on his mind. Even though had been weeks since the death of his twin, he missed her every minute of the day. He could still smell her blood. It was thick in his nostrils and throat, but mostly inside his head. She was his rib and the reason he breathed each day. Ever since they were kids, he put her before himself. But when the time came to die for her, he failed.

He remembered everything they went through with their T-Jones. The fights were the worst. He used to let Rachel beat his ass to save hers from the monster they called mama. He bit into his inner jaw as his mind drifted back to the unforgiving day.

"Shut the fuck, bitches. I swear I hate y'all. Lisa, look at these two muthafuckas. You know what. I want to see y'all fight again. Whoever cries first, I'm beating the shit out of them," Jochebed screamed.

Hideous was used to the beatings by now. But his sister was so weak and fragile. He put his head down, knowing he couldn't hit the one person that loved him unconditionally. He knew what he had to do. And so did Rachel. She let a tear fall, then raised her fist and punched him right in the face. He took it like a G. She caught him again, but with a solid left jab that made him grit his teeth. The lessons he'd been teaching her were paying off.

"So, lil bitch, you not gon' hit this hoe back? I swear you a bitch. See, yo' sperm donor used to beat my ass," she said, pointing her finger in his face.

He knew what was coming next, so when she swung a wild punch, he easily slipped inside of it, catching her off guard.

Jochebed started to clap her hands together. "I'm impressed. So, you think you did some?" She turned her attention to Rachel and threw a haymaker right to her eye, sending her staggering back in severe pain.

"You better teach her what you are learning. Because she gon' take yo ass-whipping from now on. Now get the fuck out my sight!"

"It's okay, Rachel. I'm not gon' let her or anybody else hurt you. I promise." He wiped the tears from her pretty face.

Every time he thought back over his childhood, it haunted him and put more rage into his heart. The only time his T-Jones showed any concern was when he or his twin had money.

When he made it back to the old neighborhood he grew up in, memories came rushing at him like an NFL linebacker. He hated to be back on that old soil, but he had nowhere else to go. Uzi Mi didn't just take his sister's life; he also took all the money he had.

Now he had to start over.

The only thing he had left was a Cuban link worth twenty-two racks, a replica of his sister's. And the Cybertruck he bought with cash.

He glanced over his shoulder and peered at Lisa Parker's house. He was still on the lookout for his old partner in crime, Shoota Face. He couldn't wait to shoot them thangz with him. The last he heard, Shoota Face was lying low in

East Dallas with a stripper bitch. Sarah had also told him her brother was hooked on drugs the dumb way.

Hideous decided to make his presence known.

He stood in front of Ms. Parker's crib. Just as he was about to ring the doorbell, he heard a sudden shriek of rubber down the street on Messa Circle. He watched as an unmarked black Dodge Charger fishtailed off the shoulder, barreled around the curve, and slammed its brakes.

Hideous palmed the grip of his Glock and drew it as he hit the driveway, ducked his head, and ran up the steps two at a time.

"Sarah, Sarah," he yelled as he pounded on the door with the barrel of the Glock.

Lisa answered the door, looking surprised as ever.

"Reuben Cash, put your hands up and get on the ground slowly. Drop your weapon. You are under arrest for the murder of Mark Anthony Sr.," came a yell from behind him.

Hideous looked over his shoulder. Down the stairs stood an ugly, bald-headed Black man with a gun pointed at him. The man was standing behind his whip, so Hideous doubted he could get a good shot off—especially since the sun was blocking his vision.

Boc. Boc. Boc.

He shoved Lisa out of the way and ran toward the back door. Mark took off after him, pushing Lisa back to the floor just as she was getting to her feet.

"Got damn! You bitches ain't gon' be putting y'all hands on me in my muthafuckin' house," she spat after them.

Mark ran straight out the open door and hopped the fence. He scanned the trees and the back alleyway but didn't see any sign of Hideous. Then he heard footsteps coming from one of the houses behind him.

Hideous was in somebody's backyard trying to get away. Unfortunately, Mark wasn't having that shit. He wasn't getting away—not today.

"Freeze."

Mark was truly determined to do something bad to him. He fired several shots that barely missed.

"Damn, this nigga fast."

He tried to keep up, but Hideous cut through a yard, and it was like he had nitro boost hooked up to his shoes or some shit.

"Stop," Mark yelled, trying to keep up or get off a clean shot.

Hideous sprinted between old, ragged houses, kicking up dirt as he ran like he had just won the lottery. Mark followed him onto the main street.

They ran down Record Crossing, passed the recreation center, and passed a line of boarded-up offices. Then suddenly Hideous took a sharp turn, cutting toward the church at the dead end.

He looked back and didn't see the opp.

The church had been abandoned for years. It was boarded up and looked like it might crumble to the ground any day. But that didn't stop him from breaking and entering.

At just about noon, Hideous emerged from the church. He figured the coast was clear since he had been hiding there since morning. He was irritable and frustrated. He crept down the street and didn't see any sign of a threat.

Wanted for murder. Broke with no money. And still trying to kill Uzi Mi.

He couldn't believe the direction his life had gone in a matter of seconds. Just a month ago he was running a strip club and was up $700K. Now he was sitting on a curb, his head buried in his hands, not knowing what to do or who to trust.

For the next couple of minutes, he sat there listening to the wind and watching cars pass by.

Damn, I miss my twin.

Rachel was all he ever had in life. He didn't know what to do without her. He was broke and wanted for murder.

He thought back to how he had gotten so lucky when Uzi Mi robbed that bank and got away easily, only to crash on his block. The bank robbery had been all over the news for days. They ran in and got away with $700K easily.

He pondered on that for a moment.

Then it hit him like a punch to the gut.

He needed to rob a bank—and fast.

But who could he trust?

He needed a team.

Right then he knew just who.

Chapter 8

Obama Runts

Hideous pulled over his Cybertruck and let it park itself. As it did, he popped in a fresh clip and hopped out once it finished parking. He stuffed his Uzi and made his way to the front entrance.

He had stayed in the abandoned church for almost an hour before making his exit. During that hour, all he could think about was getting to the money. He knew he needed money to go after a nigga like Uzi Mi.

He had heard Uzi Mi was running with his cousin's gang. They were calling themselves Uptown Gang, and they had Miami on lock. Most of them were being targeted in a multi-agency operation that resulted in numerous arrests on charges including RICO and drug-related offenses. They were all dreaded up, making it harder for Dade County authorities.

Bam. Bam.

Hideous pounded on Butt-Butt's door, waiting for her to open it. When she finally did, a thick cloud of smoke hit his nose from the shit she was smoking. She stood there half naked in just a yellow G-string, no top. Her hair was styled in a purple mohawk, and she had Fenty lip gloss on her Meagan Good-shaped lips.

"Is that him, bitch?"

"Yeah." She passed the blunt to Bunz, and Bunz inhaled the weed into her system. They both stared at Hideous like they wanted to fuck him right there. It had been two and a half weeks since they had seen or fucked him outside of DG's.

"Nigga, where the fuck you been?" Bunz said, standing there looking at him with pure lust.

Unlike Butt-Butt, Bunz was completely naked. She had her hair cut short like Amber Rose.

Hideous looked around the enormous condo and had to give them credit where credit was due. They were on top of their shit, living like movie stars. The last time he heard, they were stripping in Houston at Splash House.

Shoutout to *Sauce Walka*.

He heard they were shaking ass all through that bitch. Money got thrown on them from major niggas in the streets. He felt bad about what he was about to ask of them, but he had to get at some munyun.

He watched as they both made their way to the white leather sofa he was sitting on. They were looking at him with lust written all over their faces.

"First, we're sorry to hear about your sister," Butt-Butt said as she looked him directly in the eyes. She could see the hurt in them.

"I'm getting through it. That's part of the reason I need y'all's help."

"Wassup, daddy? What you need? Whatever it is, we got you. Right, Bunz?"

"Of course." Bunz stood and walked her big-ass booty to the mini bar. Hideous couldn't help but stare at how it jumped from side to side like a tennis ball.

"So, what you need?" Butt-Butt asked again.

"Money!" he shot back quickly.

Bunz looked over her shoulder. She had just done a line of coke on a paper plate when Hideous said money. Nothing got her pussy wetter than money.

"What you saying—you need some money? I can give you that," Butt-Butt said.

"Naw, I need y'all help."

After he explained what he needed from them, they both went silent.

Until Bunz said, "So you want us to help you rob a bank?"

"Technically speaking, a check-cashing store. I got the perfect one that's ducked off. All we gotta do is get this money," Hideous said.

All three of them lifted their red plastic cups.

***

Detective Mark D. Anthony couldn't believe he had let Hideous get away. He took his frustration out on a blue-eyed, big-titty white bitch. He had her legs straight up in the air, killing her insides.

"Oh my gawd, you are hurting me," Amanda said. She was on parole. She had gotten caught with some dirty syringes and was fucking and sucking for her freedom.

Mark was in his own hateful world.

"I had him—I had him," he repeated over and over out loud.

He watched his dick as it invaded Amanda's tight space. She tried to push him away, but that only made him go harder in her pussy. He was going so hard and deep she could feel his balls slapping against her ass as he pounded and pounded.

Wham. Wham. Wham.

"Fuck," she screamed and came all over his dick for the umpteenth time. "Please—oh shit. I can't take no more." She shook her head from side to side, trying her hardest not to lose it.

After a few more hard strokes, Mark finally pulled out and nutted all over her face like she meant nothing to him—across her face, chin, and big-ass tits.

"What the fuck is wrong with you?" Amanda said, wiping the nut off her skin.

Mark got up and dug in his jeans pockets. He grabbed his wallet and pulled out twenty dollars.

"Get yo' shit and get the fuck out."

"What? It's two o'clock. Where am I supposed to go?"

Mark started picking up her things. He walked over to the door and threw all her shit outside.

"Get the fuck out my house."

"Go to hell," Amanda screamed.

That's when Mark lost it.

He attacked her like a hungry wolf. He grabbed her by the hair and dragged her out the door, while she was kicking and screaming. He threw her out butt naked. He didn't give a fuck.

Later he sat on the bed, fully aware of what he was becoming. He was drinking like his old man and chasing hookers just like him. He looked at the bottle in his hand and feared he was going to lose everything he had worked so hard to gain.

He thought about the son of a bitch who took the one person he looked up to.

He couldn't wait to catch up with Hideous.

Chapter 9

Cashing Out

Butt-Butt was pacing back and forth across the living room. Hideous was going to be there any minute. Every time she heard a car, she would run to the window to see if it was him.

She walked over to the mini bar and sniffed a line of coke that was laid out on the marble counter. Then she headed to Bunz's bedroom. She opened the door and stood in the doorway, looking at her bitch naked as the day she was born, loading up the guns Hideous had given them.

"Bitch, you're actually ready for this?" Butt-Butt asked.

"Hell yeah, bitch. You're not?"

"Yeah, but I ain't gon' lie—I'm scared as fuck." Butt-Butt laughed.

"Bitch, we gon' just get this munyun and we gon' turn up. What's the worst that can happen? We shake our asses every day for killers and robbers. Damn, let's get some money too. A bitch gets tired of shaking her ass for these broke-ass niggas that just wanna get a free feel." Bunz was going the fuck off.

"You're right. Let's get this money."

Somewhere On I-75

"I'll be at the club later on. Let me get this money first. I really need you and the others, Sabrina." He drove the Cybertruck like an old-school Chevy. He was determined to get all that he had lost back. He had to admit he went downhill and gave up on life after losing his twin sister. He just didn't want to live anymore. But now he had snapped out of it. He wanted to feel what he used to feel when he had all that money. He had to get back on his shit.

Twenty minutes later, he pulled up and double-parked in front of Butt-Butt's building. He called her for the umpteenth time. He finally watched as Bunz and Butt-Butt walked out the building, toting a lot of ass.

They both rocked black booty shorts, black halter tops, and black Air Force 1s. They both climbed into the Tesla and shut the door. He pulled off down the street, turned on the first corner, and didn't drive too far before parking at the Park Lane Station.

Butt-Butt and Bunz looked at each other with confused expressions, especially when he pulled up next to a white Mercedes-Benz.

"What's going on, Hideous?" Butt-Butt asked, trying to conceal the gun she had.

"We 'bout to get this money. I'll tell y'all when we get there. Just get in the car."

He got behind the wheel and drove the Benz into traffic. The only thing on his mind was *dead presidents*.

Forty-five Minutes Later

Hideous pulled up and parked in front of an old grocery store. His eyes made contact with one thing and one thing only: the check-cashing store.

He hopped out, got in the back seat, and said, "Y'all know what to do."

At eight-thirty that night, Jeff Houston was about to close the security gate on the corner of Bruton and Master. He started sliding the metal back from the plexiglass window when he saw two thick bitches hopping out of an all-white, big-body Mercedes-Benz a few feet from the entrance of the store.

"I hope you're not closing, sir," Bunz said, carrying a fake baby in her arm that Hideous had surprised her with. The bitch even had a blanket.

"I'm sorry—we're closed. The manager's putting things away as we speak."

"Please, sir, we have nowhere to go. I got to cash this child-support check," Bunz said as she approached him quickly.

"I wish I could help . . ." was the last thing Jeff managed to say.

What happened next was not what he expected.

Bunz threw the baby doll to the floor and held a gun pointed directly at his face.

"Please, don't hurt me," he cried, both hands raised like an eager kid ready to answer the teacher's question.

At that precise moment, he saw another figure hopping out the back of the Benz, carrying an Uzi submachine gun in his hand.

"Walk yo' bitch-ass back inside," Hideous spat with venom.

Jeff fiddled with the gate and the double locks. His hands were shaking as he swung the door open. Hideous walked him deliberately and quickly past Bunz and Butt-Butt, right to the back of the store where the lines led to the teller windows.

"Go tie the bitch up in the office," Hideous said, and both women scrambled.

"Daddy, get in here quick," Bunz shouted from the office.

There was a safe in the office.

"Open this muthafucka!" Hideous told the lil' Mexican lady.

She was shaking badly, like it was below twenty degrees in that small office. She could barely hold the key. She poked at the lock until she finally got the key into the small hole.

It opened with one twist.

She swung the safe door open. Hideous focused on the envelopes filled with money.

He stuffed at least twenty envelopes into his Goyard bag while Butt-Butt and Bunz picked up money from different drawers.

He knew he had to kill the manager and Jeff. They had seen enough of their faces to pick Butt-Butt and Bunz out of a lineup.

So he made it quick.

He shot them each in the head twice, then located the camera feed and destroyed any evidence of them ever being there.

Later…

Hideous grabbed the bottle of champagne and popped the top. He held it up in the air above his head. "Rest in peace, Rachel." He grabbed it by the neck and turned it up. He took a long swig, then sat it down on the table. He was at the newest strip club in the city called: **Pink House Dallas**. It was making a lot of noise in the city.

Pink House had all the bad bitches, from DeSoto to the Agg, to the Funk—to the Cliff. He watched the strippers; all of them were naked and shaking ass. It seemed like to him every bitch in that bitch had ass shots. Every bitch in there looked like an Instagram model.

It had been weeks since he stepped foot into a club. After shooting up DG's and unaliving two muthafuckas, he opened up *Tipz*, which he ran out of a row house in the basement. But he unalived three niggas and hadn't been back to a club scene since. He was really tripping for being at one now. But he had to get his mind off his twin. She wasn't coming back. She was gone forever. Plus, he had business to conduct with three more women that eventually added to his bag. He had to rebuild himself. He was a killer by nature. And he was about to turn back up. He hit well tonight. Over $90 racks.

As he sat there replaying murders he had committed and nightmares of being a young killer, a thick waitress by the name of Taylor Huff stepped up, invading his personal space. He looked her over. She had thighs, hips and an ass like a stripper. She was a bad bitch. Too bad to be anybody's waitress. She smiled at him with lust in her eyes.

"Can I get you anything?" Her ass poked out like the back of a station wagon.

"I'm good right now, ma, but you can give a nigga a lap dance."

"Now, you know I'm not allowed to do that."

"I know, but you the only bitch I want to spend my money with." He pulled out a wad of stolen blood money and counted out two racks and told her to bring him back ones.

"How about I just pull up a chair, and we chop it up for a while."

"I prefer you to sit in my lap," he said, squeezing the shit out of her big ol' booty.

She obeyed.

She sat that big ol' thang in his lap and looked back and said, "You gon' get a bitch fired."

"If that happens you can come work for me."

"Boy, where you work? You a drug dealer or some shit?" She grabbed his bust-down and examined the picture. "She is pretty, who is it?"

"My twin sister. She died two weeks ago."

"Awww, I'm so sorry." She looked back at him, pouting her bottom lip.

"Fuck all that. Let a nigga see what you can do."

Taylor stood to her feet making that fat ass clap. All Hideous could think about is Jell-O.

For the next hour, Hideous and Taylor Huff chopped it up. Once she left, he looked at his iPhone. It was one-something and Sabrina still wasn't there. Just when he was about to leave, he spotted Roxy and Beauty, with Sabrina in tow.

"Y'all late as fuck," he said, dropping a hundred-dollar tip on the table and quickly leading Sabrina out into the night breeze by her elbow. The others followed behind.

"Nigga, you told me at one," Sabrina spat back in her hood-rat voice, waving her hand in his face as they crossed the parking lot.

"I said twelve," Hideous shot back as they headed West towards his Cybertruck. "I told you I needed to peep out this diamond store in Frisco."

"Do I look like a kid to you?" Sabrina asked, ripping her elbow out of his hand. She looked him up and down. It had been weeks since he'd last seen her. She still looked good as hell.

"Not at all. Just be on point in the morning."

Chapter 10

Money on my Mental

Early the next morning…

Six blocks west of the Ascot Diamonds Dallas, a fifteen-foot *All My Sons* moving truck pulled up on a quiet street of Addison. The driver, a big-booty ass yellow bitch, in green *All My Sons* hoody and black tights, jumped down from the truck. At the back of the truck, she threw up the container door, lowered the loading ramp, and disappeared inside.

In the window of the luxury boutique, she saw a brooch shaped like a peacock with plumage made from precious stones. Sabrina smiled at Hideous. He felt kind of bad for not bringing Butt-Butt or Bunz, but they'd made 10 apiece and were satisfied on their way to Jamaica right now.

The thin walls of the trailer hid the nightmare that was about to unfold within minutes. Roxy and Beauty were up. They pulled up in front of the store in the same white Benz that had bloody handprints all over it. He watched them from the other side of the street, across from the jewelry store and the restaurant. He felt nervous, but in a positive way. He felt invigorated. He felt dangerous and volatile, and he liked the feeling of empowerment. Plus, he needed the money.

The marble floor inside looked clean enough to eat from. The heels of Beauty's long black leather boots clacked on the marble floor. She hiked up her long skirt just to tease Roxy, showing off her fat, jiggly ass. It was all part of the plan.

"Welcome, can I help you?" a big-titty petite white woman asked. Her name was Heather. She tapped the glass that Beauty was examining. Inside the display cases, each piece shined like a flashlight.

"I'm in love with that one," Beauty said, tapping the glass.

"It's a lovely piece. Would you like to see it?" Heather said, pulling out a thin white glove to unlock the case and extract a six-carat diamond set in platinum. The whole set alone was worth a million dollars. Even though these black hoes did not strike Heather as likely buyers, she'd seen stranger things there. Beauty slipped a ring onto her finger and stared down at her hand.

"It looks beautiful on you." Heather leaned in.

"How much is this piece?"

"I believe that one is $230,000, but I've to double check."

Beauty held the ring up to her face. She couldn't believe she had a ring that cost more than everything she owned wrapped around her finger.

Meanwhile, another white woman with big tits was showing Roxy a pale-yellow princess-cut stone when two masked gunmen ran inside with automatic weapons drawn. Sabrina hurried to the armed security, disarmed and zip-tied him.

Unbeknownst to Hideous, a package arrived that morning with an armed escort. Heather signed for the delivery that was insured for five million dollars. The guards showed her the necklace before they placed it in the safe. A twenty-carat pear-shaped stone that was shipped from Dubai.

Hideous ran over and hit Beauty with the butt of the gun, drawing blood immediately. He then pointed it at Heather. She was scared shitless. He gently grabbed her by the hair and steered her to the back. The second they moved, the air filled with the violent spray of shattering glass. "Take me to the safe, bitch."

He had one black-gloved hand on his gun, the other on the back of her neck. Heather unlocked the door and went straight for the safe, a head-high custom piece. She knew the combination like her date of birth.

She was shaking so much that Hideous moved his hand from her neck to her arm. She got the combination right this time. The steel bolts in the door retracted and Hideous moved her to the side. Out came the necklace and 22 diamond rings arranged by color and weight. And $300 thousand dollars. He done struck gold for the second time. First, the robbery of Uzi Mi, and now this. He saw the neat rows in his mind's eye as the rings and necklaces were being put into bags by his girls. Heather sat down beside the gaping safe.

He zip-tied Heather and the other big-titty bitch's hands behind their back.

Excitement rushed through his veins. They had stolen a piece worth $5 million. All he had to do now was find a buyer willing to pay what he had to offer. He knew exactly who would buy it all: Suwoo Chan.

Chapter 11

Unfinished Business

Over the years Hideous had done many things for the man his father stole a bunch of money from. Unbeknownst to him, he had no idea what his father had really done. Hideous always believed his father worked as a shooter or some shit for Suwoo Chan. Since he was a kid, he heard so many stories of his father's legacy. The streets said he used to twist shit up and leave a trail of bodies scattered all over the metroplex.

His T-Jones never talked about his father or told him how she sold off her kids for a debt their father owed on his death bed. All she ever said about him was how much she hated him. She never mentioned how she was the reason his father died. How she set him up for the $100k that was put on his head.

Hideous's fingers were itching with excitement as he stared at the $5 million, twenty-carat pear-shaped stone. He knew for a fact he was about to get the money he needed to get at Uzi Mi.

"Baby, you sho you got a warrant for murder?" Sabrina asked as she walked into the bedroom, holding her Apple laptop in her hand, blowing his thoughts in the wind.

"I'm positive. Why, wassup?"

"Well, I took a look like you asked me to do, and I ain't see shit."

A sinister smile came across his face. Hideous knew right then his past had come back to haunt him. He had to find that fake-ass officer and put a bullet in his head. But before he could even think about that, he had unfinished business he had to take care of. He had to meet with Suwoo Chan to get rid of the blood diamonds he'd managed to get.

"Where are you going now?" Sabrina asked when Hideous made his way out of the bedroom.

"To sell these diamonds and get our money."

She loved the sound of that.

The sky was filled with evil, and the streets were filled with darkness. In another hour or so, things would start to pick up: the hookers, the drug dealers making transactions, the early-morning sanitation crews. His meeting with Suwoo Chan wouldn't be for another couple of weeks. He just had to get out of that house with Sabrina. She had a smart-ass mouth and was very controlling.

By the time he made it back to Sabrina's crib, she was sitting on the floor while Beauty braided her hair. They both were rocking mugs on their pretty faces.

"Did you handle that unfinished business you said you had to handle with the diamonds and our money?"

"I hope we get paid soon," Beauty mumbled under her breath. The Lord knew she needed it.

Hideous's iPhone brought his mind back to peace, because he was 'bout to go dumb on both of them. He looked down at the screen and saw it was Laei Chan. He was Suwoo Chan's son.

"Laei, what it do? Haven't heard from ya in a while."

"I know. I'm sorry to hear about my Rachael." He always had a crush on Rachael, just like Hideous always had a thing for his sister.

"How your sister been?"

"Matter of fact, she right here. You want to speak to her?"

"Naw, I need to speak to yo' father. Where he at?"

Laei looked past the clear blue water that surrounded the all-white yacht floating smoothly across the coast. He looked at his powerful father standing there at the bottom of the deck with his two Black wives. “I got ya; we on vacation. He down there with my T-Jones. I’ll have him call you back ASAP.”

After Hideous disconnected the call with Laei, he sat on the edge of the bed and laid the precious jewels across the sheet. He knew Suwoo Chan was getting up in age and Laei was going to take over, but then again, Ling was more G’ed out than her little brother.

Hideous was scanning over all the jewelry when Sabrina walked into the room. She was a bad bitch, no doubt, with a lot of ass that jiggled more than Cardi B’s in a music video. As soon as she closed the door, she picked back up with that fly-ass mouth of hers. “Who you were on the phone with, trick? You come over here and put me and my bitches’ life in danger. Where is our bread?” she vented with her hands folded across her chest.

“You on some mo’ shit. You and them same bitches came to me with not a damn thang in y’all pockets, begging to work at my club . . . then I paid y’all the night my sister got killed—more than y’all ever made popping coochies. Please miss me with all that other shit. How I see it, y’all hoes owe me.”

“We owe you, really?”

“I’m not ’bout to go back and forth with you. Check this shit out. I’m gon’ pay y’all when I sell the diamonds.” He tried to push past her, but she wasn’t having it. There wasn’t any way she was letting them diamonds out of her sight. She stared into his eyes. She had never given him any pussy before; mostly she ever did was just tease him. On the cool, he never tried to get it.

She untied her sundress and let it slide slowly down her naked body to the floor around her feet. He just looked. He knew he was not one of the prettiest niggas she’d been with, and no amount of money or power could change that unalterable fact. He had spent his entire life as the ugly kid on the block. It actually hurt his own eyes to look at his ugly self. He knew she was only doing this for the diamonds. And he had learned, when he took Uzi Mi's money, that money and power changed the way people look at you. She was amazing. He had seen her naked plenty of times back at the club he owned, but he'd never seen it being showcased quite like this. She was a gangsta.

He couldn't remember how their livesintertwined with each other. Then he remembered Caprice—rest her soul—introduced him to Sabrina on the opening night of his Club Tipz. Their relationship grew once she helped him get to Uzi Mi. After that day, she'd been down with him along with her two friends. After the death of his sister, they reached out to him, but he never reached back until now.

She stepped up to him. She was eager to see the big ol' dick Caprice used to brag about. She stuck her hand down his pants and almost screamed. She stroked it back and forth as she looked him dead in the eyes.

It was huge.

When she finally pulled it out, her eyes almost popped out of her head, cartoon-like. She squatted down to the floor with her legs wide open. She grabbed his enormous dick with no hands. With all mouth, she started to suck his dick viciously. She bounced up and down with the dick deep in her mouth. She pulled her sexy lips away from the dick real slow-like, watching all that could fit come out of her mouth like an anaconda.

She ran her tongue up the long shaft as she polished the head of his dick with her wet mouth. She felt his hand in her hair, gently guiding her as she took him all the way down her throat—no gag reflex at all. She really did this shit. She cupped his balls in her hand and let him fuck her mouth.

Uck. Uck. Uck. Uck.

After Sabrina had eaten the dick like a full-course meal, Hideous sat on the edge of the bed, enjoying her fat-ass booty bounce up and down on his twelve-inch dick. She turned her head and smiled with pain written all over her face. He couldn't believe she was taking all his dick like a champ. She even freestyled, bouncing up and down on the dick sideways on the bed.

Smack. Smack. Smack.

She was giving him the ride of his life. She fucked him with ferocity, slamming her big ass on his dick like she was trying to break it. His nut was building and sending him over the edge. He felt her fat pussy throbbing around his dick, squeezing him. The sound of her ass smacking against his flesh continued to fill the air.

Smack. Smack. Smack.

She looked over her shoulder when Hideous fell back on the bed and closed his eyes. She just kept bouncing like a kid in a funhouse. "Yes, daddy, yes, daddy. This some good-ass dick. I can't wait to tell the others," she cried over and over. Just when she was popping that pussy and gripping his dick like a glove, he shot a load deep inside her. They were foolish not to wear protection. She looked back at him with a smirk, laughing to herself on the inside. *I knew you couldn't handle this wet-ass pussy.* She made her ass cheeks jump, one cheek at a time, on the dick.

Sabrina collapsed on the bed next to him. "Roxy and Beauty gon' want some of that dick, too. After you sell the diamonds, we can all just sit around and fuck all day. How will you like that?"

Hideous was speechless.

Chapter 12

Back to the Money

Two weeks after the diamond store heist, Hideous finally managed to set up a private meeting with the infamous Suwoo Chan, the main underboss of the Red Dragon Cartel.

The only problem was: the meeting was arranged for three months away. He needed the money now. He watched from afar as Bunz, wearing a pair of boyshorts, knocked on the thick glass of the door. "Help. Please. My car is burning and my homegirl is in there," she screamed at the security guard on the other side.

It was nine o'clock in the morning. Bunz had her hands on the sides of her head, her body on full display for the security guard. Her nipples poked clear through her shirt, and the bottom of her ass cheeks slipped from her tiny shorts. The security guard was mesmerized. Of course, he would help her. She played her part well.

The guard was a big, mean-looking Black man with a bald head. He looked like Deebo off *Friday*. He stood at the window, looking out at the white Benz; it was pouring black smoke from underneath the hood.

Another big-booty bitch was bending over like she was trying to look under the car for the cause of the problem. She also had on some little-ass shorts that did very poorly at covering any of her big ass up.

"What's going on?" the white, blonde clerk asked. She walked to the window and stood next to the guard. The upscale jewelry store had barely been open a few minutes. "Is their car on fire? Oh my gawd, you have to help them. I'll call the fire department."

"No need. I'll handle it. Get back to work. Probably a blown engine," Eddie said, making his way out of the store.

"Please, help us. My car just started smoking and my homegirl is trapped inside." Bunz turned and jogged a foot or two toward the white Benz, throwing ass everywhere like Serena Williams in a tennis match.

As soon as Eddie reached the car, Hideous popped up from the backseat with a shotgun aimed at his face. "You know what it is." Hideous stepped out, wearing a wig and dressed in drag. He escorted Eddie back inside the high-end jewelry store at gunpoint.

"Down. Down. Down," he yelled, pointing the shotgun in the faces of the two store clerks. Butt-Butt and Bunz finally entered the golden-lit store, now with masks on their faces. They went from the front to the back, smashing display cases with sledgehammers and crowbars. In minutes, they had five display cases shattered to bits and pieces. They were scooping high-end jewelry up faster than they had done anything in their lives.

They were out the door within three minutes, with Hideous right behind them. They headed west, trying not to draw any attention—but that was hard to do when both their asses were jiggling like crazy. They walked right past the smoked-out Benz, ignoring the people out on the streets trying to see what was going on, none of them knowing the jewelry store had just been robbed.

Hideous wasn't worried about it. They now rocked backpacks with Nikon cameras around their necks like tourists. He was still dressed like a woman. He led his team to the train station by the American Airlines Center, walking shoulder to shoulder as they disappeared onto an incoming train heading toward downtown.

When the Green Line made it to the West End Station, Hideous and the rest of them hurried to his Cybertruck. He'd planned it out well. "Wassup? Why you smiling so hard?" he asked Butt-Butt.

"Because we just hit big, Daddy."

"Hell yeah, we did. When we cash out, we might not have to shake no more ass for a while," Bunz said with a wicked smile. "Daddy, when are we going after Uzi Mi?"

Hideous's jaw started to twitch at the sound of the nigga's name. "As soon as we sell these diamonds," he replied, swerving through traffic.

"Well, I know this one nigga that works as a bouncer back at the club. He be trying to fuck on me and Bunz, right? He be bragging, saying he used to work for Uzi Mi. I never believed shit he said, though; the nigga lies so much."

Skirrrrkkkk. Hideous pulled the car over so fast he almost caused an accident. He looked at them with hatred in his eyes. "Why y'all just now telling me this? The nigga's name is Black Rhino?"

"Baby, I swear we didn't know."

"He's one of the niggas that kidnapped my sister. When's the next time y'all gon' see that bitch-made ass nigga?"

"This weekend," Butt-Butt shot back quickly, her head down.

"Keep that nigga busy. He gon' bleed this weekend."

Bunz recognized the seriousness in his tone and knew blood was about to be shed.

Chapter 13

A New Enemy

Fat Mama was sitting inside the packed strip club, surveying the club with a discerning eye. She was a big-booty, short chocolate bitch, only 4'9" but carrying a thick 135 pounds on her. She was built like a dark-skinned Cardi B. She had so much ass that it jiggled with every step.

Since putting her lil' brother, Lil' Judah on, she didn't necessarily have to strip, not with the money they were making robbing niggas. She did so it she could one day run into Hideous.

As she sat there, mesmerized by the various big-money hustlas in the building, she saw one of her younger brother's old partnas. She knew he was the same age as Mark, but at that moment, all she saw was green. Sitting on the side of Lil' T was his old man, Big T. Big T was *that* nigga in Old East Dallas. He was a big-time hustla, and the ice on his neck and mouth spoke for his success.

She knew she couldn't get to him personally; he had a dozen niggas sitting with him. But with an ass like hers, she knew she could get to the President of the United States. His son would be as easy as taking candy from a baby.

She remembered when they were young, Mark used to beat the shit out of Lil' T for always staring at her ass. Now it was bigger and she was badder. She was about to see what he was about.

"Damn, would you look at that," Big T said, nodding toward Fat Mama. She had an ass like famous IG model Zmeena Orr and looked like a dark-skinned Kylie Jenner before the fame. Noticing the main eye she wanted was on her, she smiled and made her way over to their table.

"Pops, that's Mark's sister. You remember Mark, right?"

"Mark? Oh, Mark—the young, wild nigga. Used to always beat yo' ass for somethin'."

"Hey, Daddy," Fat Mama said as she walked up to their table, her voluptuous booty bouncing like a basketball for them. She wanted them to see her whole; she loved being naked. She looked at Lil' T and smiled. "Don't I know you?" she asked, knowing damn well she did. At that moment, she felt a strong pair of hands grab her arm and pull her toward them. It was the old man.

"You don't got no manners?"

Big T was tall and muscular, Black as tar. She yanked her arm away from him, playing her part well. "Nigga, why you grabbing me like that? I don't know you."

"Bitch, I'm Big T. I know you heard of me. I was the first nigga in the city with a Bentley."

Fat Mama rolled her eyes. "I never heard of you." She looked back at Lil' T. He couldn't believe she handled his old man like that in front of everybody; nobody ever talked to him in that manner before. "Don't I know you?"

"Yeah. Your brother Mark is my nigga."

Fat Mama smiled, revealing her deep dimples. "Yeah, I remember you. You and my brother stayed into it because you couldn't keep your eyes off my ass."

"And a nigga still can't."

"Oh, okay. I can sit in yo' lap, then."

Lil' T looked over at his pops to ask what he should do. Big T nodded his approval. Fat Mama eased her Zmeena Orr-shaped ass down into his lap. His dick instantly rocked up. She purposely grinded her exposed ass on his crotch.

"You ain't young no mo'. And you don't got to worry about my brother. What you getting into after you leave here? We can probably catch up on old times," she said in a sexy-ass tone, getting straight to the point.

"We can do whatever." She spun around on his lap and faced his pops. She locked eyes with him and saw the lust. Meanwhile, Lil' T looked down and saw nothing but ass grinding back and forth on his member. Her ass was so juicy he could no longer see the yellow string that was part of her G-string. She started bouncing up and down, smirking as watched the frustration build in Big T. He couldn't take it no more. He pushed her legs apart, cut through her, running the blade of his hand up the inside of her thighs. He cupped her pussy. She stifled a moan.

"I'm going to fuck the shit out of you."

"Is that right?" she asked with a sexy-ass smile.

He nodded, trying to slide a finger in her pussy, but she smacked his hand away and continued to slowly bounce that ass up and down on his son's lap. She left Lil' T's mind wandering. "Get at me when you are alone and not with a bunch of people, especially your old man. He gives me the creeps." She leaned back so nobody else would hear her. "You might just get lucky and get some of this good pussy."

With that, she stood up with an ass fat as an elephant's. She looked back at him and smiled, walking off like a model on a runway. She purposely threw that ass in different directions. Each cheek bounced seductively, catching father and son's undivided attention.

Fat Mama liked to bounce her fat ass around. Her ass shook like loose car parts every time she took a step. She had the tightest pussy ever. If she gave that thang to either Big T or Lil' T, she was gon' have her way.

She stopped at the bar, standing pigeon-toed on her thick legs. She started talking to a bartender named Sleepy, who got that name because her eyes always stayed low and slanted. As they chopped it up about Big T and his son, a big

Black bouncer snuck up behind Fat Mama. His enormous hand came down and gave her round ass a hard *smack.* He watched her left cheek jiggle, then brought his other hand down on the opposite cheek.

"Damn, I love my job," he spat as she made that fat ass of hers clap to the Zillionaire Doe. She knew exactly who was behind her, breathing down her neck. Black Rhino was either fuckin' all the strippers at Dallas Cabaret or trying—and with Fat Mama, he was definitely trying. She wasn't like the other strippers trying to win a boss nigga. Her little brother, Lil' Judah, was already that. Her sole purpose was to one day run into the one man she hated more than anyone in this world.

When she looked back, her heart started beating harder than Grambling vs. PV's *Battle of the Bands*. She had to be seeing shit. There wasn't any way Hideous had just walked through the door of her club—and he had those two hoes she couldn't stand with him: Bunz and Butt-Butt. Revenge was essential for her peace of mind. She wanted him dead, and bad.

Her eyes followed him and the two strippers to a VIP area located close to the stage. There was no way in hell she was letting him leave her sight. She rushed to the locker room to retrieve her iPhone and throw on her yellow and black tank top that read *Anti-Broke Niggas*. She freshened up and headed straight back to a spot where she could see Hideous as she called her brother, Cain.

"What it do, big sis?" Cain answered on the fourth ring.

"Boy, where you at?"

"Chilling over here at the spot with James and Mark."

"Where the whip?"

"Judah tripping about his shit. You know how he is about his car."

"This nigga up here tripping with me."

"Who? I'll fuck that nigga up!" His voice came booming through the phone as if he were on speaker.

“Get your brothers and meet me at the club. Bring all the glizzies. Judah probably over there with Milky Way thot-ass.”

“Okay, big sis, I got ya. Keep that pussy nigga there by all means. What you want us to do about your son?”

She took a long sigh. She’d forgotten all about her six-year-old son for a second. The nigga who took his father away was only a couple of feet away. “Take him to Mama’s.”

After she disconnected the call, she made her way over to VIP. The two strippers Hideous came with were long gone, shaking their asses for a baller or two. Fat Mama stepped into the VIP room, her ass bouncing side-to-side like an impact drill. Hideous was so absorbed in watching Black Rhino that he didn’t see her at first. When he finally did, his eyes almost popped out of his head, cartoon-like. Their eyes met. Nothing was said. She lifted her shirt up over her juicy titties and held it there, standing directly in front of him. Those mouth-watering tits were bouncing around, hardening his dick in a matter of seconds.

With long black hair that framed her pretty face and curled softly down her back in a neat ponytail, she could have been a model. But attractive as she was, she wasn’t at all stuck up. Her hazel eyes seemed to look way down inside you. Her moist, voluptuous lips often curved into a smile that showed her perfect white teeth.

He was surprised when she walked up and asked if he wanted a lap dance. She didn’t give him time to answer. She turned around and bent over—losing her panties first—and spread her juicy cheeks with both hands. She smacked her ass in his face again, making sho’ she kept his undivided attention.

Smack. Smack. Smack.

He clearly didn’t know who she was, but she knew exactly who he was. And he was going to die tonight. But first, she had to get him comfortable. She looked back at him while her ass had a mind of its own, bouncing violently like waves in the ocean. Her huge cheeks bounced nonstop from side to side like a yo-yo. She stopped suddenly, making just the right cheek bounce, then both of them together.

Her big ass flapped like butterfly wings, literally flapping everywhere. Hideous was at a total loss for words; all he could do was stare dumbly as he devoured those deliciously rounded cheeks. She left him with a king-size boner tenting the front of his pants. From the corner of her eye, she saw him glance down at his own erection. The tip of her tongue darted out, moistening her alluring lips.

Except for a small light, it was dark in the VIP. He knew he had bigger shit to do than lusting after a big-booty stripper—like catching up with Black Rhino—but he had Butt-Butt and Bunz seducing the bouncer for him. When the time was right, he was gon' make his move. Until then, he watched as Fat Mama hopped back on her feet, her ass moving like water.

She had Hideous feeling like he was on a roller-coaster ride, especially when she parked that big thang on his lap. She wanted to puke when she felt his inches. She inhaled sharply when he grabbed her titties aggressively and stroked them. Her brain was in a whirlpool. She wanted, right then and there, to kill him.

She stood back up, making that ass go crazy with each movement. She was making it clap without even trying. She looked over her shoulder to take a quick peek and saw Hideous watching her intently. She stomped her six-inch heel down hard, turning up for a check.

Hideous's eyes turned cold when he saw Black Rhino. The bouncer was leaving the club with Butt-Butt and Bunz. Right then, he knew playtime was over. He pulled out a wad of money thicker than a roll of toilet paper. He stood and peeled off four crisp $100 bills.

"Wait, where you going? I thought you was having a good time with me," Fat Mama said, putting her hand down his pants. She gasped when she felt the heat and the weight of what was inside. "Boy."

"I got to handle some shit. We'll catch back up soon."

"But I want you to stay here with me," she said seductively, pulling him over to an empty booth.

She dropped to her knees. She knew she had to keep him there until her brothers arrived. She pulled out his huge dick and spat on the tip, licking it like a starving cat. His dick responded to the lip service she was giving it. She sucked him wild and sloppy, trying to deep-throat, but it was just too much. She tried, though. She even placed both hands on his knees, pushing down so the dick could go deeper in her mouth. At first, she thought she might succeed, but this nigga's dick was enormous; she could only take in half. What she could fit, she sucked industriously while stroking the rest.

When she finally let it fall out of her mouth, she gasped. She swallowed it back in when she noticed he was trying to leave again. She bobbed her head back and forth like a hundred times. *I'm going to kill my brothers,* she thought. It shouldn't have taken that long to get them together.

She reached up and squeezed his balls. "You like that, Daddy?" She rubbed his humongous dick all over her face, determined to kill his ass tonight. She turned sideways and started to lick the shaft.

Uck. Uck. Uck. Uck. She made loud slurping sounds as his dick slid in and out of her mouth, smooth and wet.

Meanwhile, outside the club in Black Rhino's blue Tahoe, his head was thrown back and his eyes were closed as the sounds of slurping echoed in his ears.

Uck-Uck-Uck-Uck-Uck-Uck. Butt-Butt and Bunz were in the back, sitting on either side with their heads buried in his lap, tag-teaming his dick. He glanced down and saw their heads moving up and down, fast as a blur. They both had their dresses pulled down over their juicy titties to their waists like a belt, but on the other side, it was pulled over nothing but ass. He played in both of their coochies, watching as they each ate up the dick like they were at *Cici's Pizza*—eating all they could eat.

"Oh, shit!" Black Rhino roared as Bunz began to push Butt-Butt's head down on the dick until her lips touched his hair. Bunz kept looking at the front door of the club, but still, there was no sign of Hideous. *Where the fuck is he?* she thought to herself.

"Bitch, I'll be right back. I got to take a piss. Let that nigga fuck you in that fat ass of yours," Bunz said, sticking a finger in Butt-Butt's ass.

When Bunz hopped out of the Tahoe, she looked back to see Butt-Butt climbing onto Black Rhino's lap. She headed back inside the club to see what the fuck had Hideous's attention.

Fat Mama now sat on the red velvet couch while Hideous stood directly in front of her with his dick in her mouth. She sucked and worked her mouth like she would a piece of Jolly Rancher. Bunz walked into the booth in a short-ass Prada dress. She was numb at first. *Not Ms. Stuck-Up. Not the bitch that was too good to socialize with strippers.*

Bunz pulled out her iPhone and recorded the scene before her. Fat Mama was going dumb. She recorded about a minute of it before putting the phone back in her purse. She cleared her throat as if they weren't in a club surrounded by muthafuckas. She grabbed both of their attention. Fat Mama looked all shy and scared. *Yeah, bitch, you got caught with dick in your mouth.*

"Nigga, we need to go. Now."

Fat Mama rocked a stank look on her face like she'd been caught by the police trying to rob a bank. Her heart twisted in a knot when she saw Hideous leave her life for the second time. She made it her business not to let it happen again as she stood to her feet. She knew she was going to be brushing the taste of him out of her mouth for a long time to come.

Outside, Bunz opened the back door to the Tahoe and saw Butt-Butt's ass moving like jelly. She was riding the shit outta Black Rhino.

"I see you finally decided to come back to join the party," Black Rhino said, peeping his head around Butt-Butt's body.

"Yeah, but I brought a familiar face with me," she said, hopping back in the Tahoe with her Glock 19 aimed at his face. He didn't know how he'd missed the gun, but then again, he was too busy trying to get some pussy.

His mouth dropped when he saw Hideous jump into the driver's seat.

"I know you remember me, nigga," Hideous spat, his cold eyes piercing him through the rearview mirror. "Enjoy the ride, because it will be your last one."

He started up the Tahoe and swerved out of the parking lot with Butt-Butt still riding dick.

Later That Night…

Fat Mama's brothers finally came barraging into the club with them Glizzys, extended mags hanging from them at the ready. They scanned the club but didn't see her anywhere. Finally, the youngest said, "There she goes."

The others looked where Mark was pointing. Fat Mama sat near VIP with her face buried in her hands. As soon as she looked up and saw her four little brothers with their guns out—and everybody looking at them crazy and scared at the same time—she instantly hopped up and stormed over to them.

She looked each of them in their cold eyes. "Y'all failed me, my nigga, real talk. Get me the fuck outta here." *I can't believe I just sucked the opp's dick,* she thought.

Lil' Judah, the oldest, took a deep breath and let it out slowly. "Big sis, we sorry for real."

"Save that shit for a bitch that gives a fuck about your sympathy," she shot back. The whole club had their eyes on her, but there wasn't shit a bitch-nigga could say. Everybody knew her brothers were making serious noise, leaving shit twisted. They stood on business. To speak about them in an ill manner meant one thing: a closed casket.

When she hopped into the front seat of her brother's Benz, she asked, "Where the fuck is my baby?"

"Milky Way got him," Lil' Judah said, turning the Benz onto the dark street.

"Big sis, we tried to get here as quick as possible," Cain said from the back.

"Y'all good. Leave it alone."

"Who was it?" Paul, the silent killer, asked the million-dollar question.

"A muthafucka that's gon' die the next time I run into him. With y'all help or without it." That was a promise she vowed to make true.

Chapter 14

My Word Is My Word

Black Rhino couldn't stop trembling. Even a man his size could feel fear, especially since he'd been lying bound on the cold stone floor. He felt like he was going to freeze to death before Hideous even got a chance to torture him.

His hands and feet were bound with heavy-duty duct tape that he'd been desperately trying to rip off, but with no success. For three days now, he had been lying in the dark in his own puddle of shit and piss. He really started to lose it when the lights flashed on. The door to the storage room came open like a hoe's legs.

At the threshold stood Hideous and the two big-booty strippers who had seduced him to this point. Hideous stepped in and knelt beside him with an Uzi in his hand. "You gon' die a slow, painful death for the pain you caused me," Hideous promised, then head-butted him in the face. His nose immediately started to leak.

"Look, I can . . ." Black Rhino was in serious pain. *I think my nose is broken.* It damn sho' felt like it. "I can help you get at Uzi Mi. I know where he is in Miami."

"Bunz, grab me that sledgehammer." Black Rhino watched in horror as the stripper grabbed a Home Depot sledgehammer with the orange handle. She handed it to the devil himself.

"Last time I heard, Uzi Mi was in Miami causing hell with the blood of my sister still on his hands—the sister you helped kidnap and kill."

"That wasn't on me! But not all his niggas went to Miami with him. He still got two niggas named Black and Flyboi out here getting rich off him, selling them fentanyl pills he's sending straight from Miami. My ears are still in the streets."

Hideous stepped back, the sledgehammer gripped in his hand. "Where can I find these two muthafuckas?" Once Rhino sang like he was trying to save himself from a life sentence, he watched as the sledgehammer came crashing toward his face like a demolition ball.

Wham.

"You better hope these addys are legit, pussy."

Blood and teeth went flying in all directions. Rhino was still spitting out bone fragments when he looked up and saw Hideous grasp the bottom handle once more, swinging with enough force to bust off a safe door.

Hideous and Butt-Butt walked out, leaving him to deal with Bunz. She carried a gallon of ice-cold water in her hand and, without warning, she poured it all over his bloody face. He wanted to die right then and there. The pain he was experiencing was just the beginning.

Hideous was riding in his Cybertruck with Butt-Butt when his iPhone rang with back-to-back calls from Sabrina. He answered when she decided to call right back.

"Nigga, where is my money?"

"Bitch, I'm doing some' right now."

"What? Laid up with a bitch?"

"Naw, bitch. Trying to make a play so I can pay yo' worrisome ass," he shot back grimly.

"Bitch, you better be by my crib with my money today." She hung up and left him looking stupid. He let out a long sigh and enjoyed the ride in his Tesla. The sound system had NBA YoungBoy sounding like a night club.

"Where we headed, bae?"

"I'm gon' have you get at Black while I try to get at Flyboi, since his trap in the Nawf is on the other side of town."

"What you want me to do?" she asked, not trying to do a lot of damage. The love she had for Hideous was growing, and she would do just about anything for him, but she loved her freedom, too.

"Put that pussy on that young nigga. And I'll do the rest."

Nawf—Dallas, Hamilton Park
10:12 at night

Hideous made several double-turns to make sure he wasn't being followed. When he got to the addy, he parked at the base of the driveway. He approached the front door and removed a lockpick gun from his back pocket. As he reached the door, he pretended to ring the bell while he worked the tool quietly. He knew from Black Rhino it was just him and his bitch, Cold Bubblez. She was a bitch from the popular show *Love & Hip Hop: Miami*—a gift from Uzi Mi.

When the lock released, he stepped inside and closed the door behind him. He paused in the entryway until his eyes grew accustomed to the darkness, then moved quietly down the hallway toward the master bedroom. The hall was lined with club pictures of Flyboi and his ACC niggas. Most were recent.

At the bedroom, the door was wide open and Flyboi was fast asleep. Crossing over to the bed, Hideous saw it was just him.

Where was his bitch?

When he looked up, he got the shock of his life. She stood naked in the doorway; her eyes lit up like the Fourth of July. His instincts took over. He aimed the Uzi at Flyboi and sprayed him down. His flesh shredded like paper. When he looked back up, the bitch was gone.

"Hell naw." Hideous took off running after her. She was almost out the door when he sprayed her back with a dozen bullet holes, leaving her shit looking like chicken pox.

"Dumb-ass bitch, messed the whole play up," Hideous growled. He needed Flyboi alive to tell him where to find Uzi Mi. Now he had to depend on Butt-Butt to get the job done. He ended up searching the house and came up with $11,000 and about 600 yellow school buses, those thick bars that could shut a nigga's whole brain down. He knew he had to get to Black.

Chapter 15

Discussing Business

"Daddy, I'm gon' fall back like you said, but this nigga got the whole block on lock. As soon as I drove into his turf, bitches started making phone calls. I'm back in the car now."

"Just go home. I'll be over there as soon as I put this nigga in the trunk. Fuck him." Hideous learned quickly that Black spread his money around the neighborhood, giving it to families in need. That type of gratitude got him the loyalty he needed; eyeballs would alert him at any given time.

But Hideous didn't give a fuck. He parked the Cybertruck and walked down Black's street, looking for trouble. People around the hood noticed him immediately, watching as he walked the notorious Latin streets of Love Field. He spotted a pretty-looking mixed breed in a T-shirt and sandals, sitting in a lawn chair propped against the front of her house. She rocked some coochie-cutter shorts that showed off her print well, but Hideous paid no attention to that. He knew she was bait.

Halfway to a heavy wooden door laced with black iron burglar bars, he looked back and saw the girl quickly get on the phone. He decided to fall back; he didn't need to draw unnecessary attention. He needed Black alive so he could feed him information on Uzi Mi.

Later that night, Hideous was behind the tint of his Cybertruck, watching the video Bunz and Butt-Butt posted on Snapchat. It was a clip of the thick stripper eating his dick back at the club. It was crazy that he'd never gotten her name, but reading the caption made his eyes light up: *Fat Mama ain't so innocent. She eating dick for free at the cab.*

Hideous read the name over and over. *Fat Mama. Fat Mama.* At that exact moment, he knew he'd almost been caught slipping with his pants down. Fat Mama wanted revenge. He remembered it all like it was yesterday. His twin, Rachael, was beating the shit out of Fat Mama when her cousin, Big Booty Susie, jumped in with Milky Way. That ended quickly when he shot and killed Mad Maxx.

Damn! he thought. He knew his past would eventually come back to haunt him. He'd killed so many: Mad Maxx, Mark D. Anthony Sr., Yella Kid, the two niggas at the club, the three at Club Tipz. The list went on—and it was about to get longer. He had to execute a plan. First, he had to deal with Bunz and Butt-Butt. He pulled out his iPhone, called them hoes, and demanded they delete the video ASAP.

Now he was back focused on Black. He sank down low in the Tesla when he saw the door to Black's trap open. Out came a nigga so Black he looked airbrushed. Even without the two bust-down Cubans that spelled out BLACK, Hideous knew it was him.

He jumped into an AMG Benz with a bad lil' bitch walking behind him. She was hugging her iPhone to her ear, talking loud. Black watched her carefully. She was beautiful, with fiery-red hair, sexy brown eyes, and huge 46DD tits he'd paid racks for. Before the money, he never pictured himself with a bitch on that level.

He wanted to pull his dick out and fuck her right there, but Frenchie had called him earlier on some weird shit. Frenchie was the young mixed breed watching his trap. She'd told him about two big-booty bitches coming by, and now a nigga in a black hoodie was lurking. He shook the feeling off. Nobody was stupid enough to try him.

"Hold up, I just saw sum'—" Black said to Mimi as she leaned over to suck his dick. He reached for his gun, but remembered it was in the trunk, buried under a duffle bag full of re-up money. It was too late anyway. Hideous popped out and aimed the Uzi at the Benz.

Budda-Budda-Budda.

Black got hit and so did Mimi. They thought they were looking at a zombie. The car light cast a faint yellow glow on Hideous's face. Black knew exactly who he was as death moved in slowly.

Hideous fired again.

Mimi fell against the side of the car, flat on her back with her pussy on full display. Once the gunfire ceased—more than twenty rounds into the Benz—the car was damaged beyond repair. Hideous searched the wreckage and found the bag of money. He looked down at Mimi, who was halfway to meeting her maker. He aimed his Uzi and fast-forwarded the meeting.

Chapter 16

Four Brothers

Cain was a different breed of violent. At 6'2 and 220 pounds of twitchy, explosive muscles, he'd been built to be the next Kenneth Murray Je. Recruiters from every Power 5 school in the country were knocking down his door, begging him to bring that middle linebacker heat to their Saturday night lights. But Cain didn't want the stadium cheers. He traded a full ride and a shot at the NFL for a glock and YN's reputation, proving his murder game was cutthroat as his blitz.

He got up from the bed and made a dash to his older sister's room. She was still asleep with his nephew, Lil' Maxx, by her side.

"What you want, boy?" Fat Mama asked as she noticed someone standing in her doorway.

"I thought you was sleep."

"Yeah, I was, but I hear everything that goes on around me."

"Is we still having that meeting?"

"You bet yo' ass we are," she said, sitting up.

"Is this about that nigga that killed Mad Maxx? Or what happened at the club?"

Old memories came rushing back to her like a bad dream, but she blocked it out of her mental like an offensive lineman. "What makes you think that?" she finally said.

"Because for the longest, you been following this nigga's social media using a fake page with a different bitch's picture. And on top of that, you been putting in a lot of work at the gun range."

She loved the fact that her baby brother was aware of so much at such a young age. He was only eighteen but had a murder game like a seasoned killer. She was going to use him and the others for her own personal gain. She wanted Hideous at her feet—she just didn't want to kill him yet. That was too easy for a nigga like him. She wanted him to suffer like his sister did. She wished she could've been there to see his face when that Nicki Minaj-looking bitch got cut down in pieces like a jigsaw puzzle.

Now, since her baby brothers were slowly installing fear in niggas' hearts around the city, she was finally going to get the revenge she'd been desperately seeking.

"We'll talk about it later tonight." With that, she turned over and held the love of her life, her six-year-old son.

Later that afternoon, Fat Mama and her four little brothers all started to gather in the living room. She was the only bitch in the room and she held each of their attention—even her son's, who was sitting in her youngest brother's lap, clutching an iPad.

Mark was the youngest; he was only fifteen. Unlike all of his other siblings, he was a pretty boy—mixed with Black and Mexican. He had good hair and a handsome face, so niggas tested his gangsta more often than the others. But he was with the shit, even though Fat Mama tried to keep him away from that side of the field.

Fat Mama convinced her four brothers that they would one day rule the streets, and that promise was being proven every day. The oldest of the four was Judah, and he was about his paper. At the age of twenty, he already had a trap that was jumping like Ja Morant and $18,000 put up. He'd been turned on to the game by his sister. She gave him two kilos of that white bitch, and he took off from there.

She looked at the gangsta he'd become and a smile spread across her face. She'd taught him to keep his circle small and deal only with family. Cain was his muscle and Paul was his shooter. Speaking of Paul, she looked over at him. He was seventeen, but he was a born killer. He didn't say much, but most killers didn't. He just sat there, praying for his next kill.

Fat Mama looked at her brothers one by one and said, "Mad Maxx been dead now for five long years, and I waited this long until y'all got a lil' older to seek my revenge on the man that took everything away from me. Hideous did that, and he's going to die. I'm not going to stop looking for him until he is dead. Y'all old enough and dangerous enough to help me take what belongs to me—and that's his soul."

"We will do anything for you," Judah said, knowing she was the reason he ate the way he did. Even before the money, she'd taken care of all of them, including her son. She managed to finish school and work. When their T-Jones got locked up, she took her spot and raised them. She even started stripping with her cousin, Big Booty Susie.

But then a lick came her way; she took it and made life better for her brothers and her son. Her mind drifted back to when her life changed for the better.

A Month Ago...

"Susie!" Fat Mama called out, her voice raised. She knocked on the door to room 214 one last time before making her way down the raggedy-ass metal stairs. Before she could hit the bottom, a man stuck his head out the door. She knew it was her cousin's nigga. *Damn, he ugly as shit,* she thought, heading back up the steps.

Shoota Face smiled when Fat Mama walked in. Unbeknownst to her, he was butt-ass naked behind the door of the funky-ass motel room. When she saw his skinny, dirty dick, she wanted to vomit.

"What the fuck! Go put some muthafuckin' clothes on . . . and damn, it stinks in here!" she spat as he stared at her booty. He remembered Susie saying all the women in her family had ass for days. She wasn't lying. "Where is my cousin?" she asked, reaching into her purse for her gun. She dared him to try her.

"In the bathroom, getting fucked up," he said with a smirk.

Fat Mama wanted to put a bullet in his head. She stormed into the bathroom, and the rumors she'd heard in the clubs were definitely true. Her favorite cousin was naked on the floor with a rope tied around her arm, high out of her mind.

Fat Mama seriously considered killing Shoota Face. To make matters worse, he stood behind her as she bent over to check Susie's pulse. She looked over her shoulder and caught him staring a hole in her ass. She gave him the finger and slammed the door in his face.

"Susie! Susie! Get yo' bitch-ass up! You in here living foul, sis."

"Huh? Who is that?" Susie looked around and groaned with exhaustion and pent-up rage. She sat there with a bad habit and a violated body, knowing what Shoota Face had done to her before she drifted off. For a moment, Susie could only stare in silence. She could hear her own ragged breathing.

Fat Mama noticed a single tear slide down her cousin's pretty face, and right then, she lost it. She stormed out of the bathroom, gun in hand. Shoota Face sat in a chair, stroking himself as he watched a video on his phone of him brutally dogging Susie.

Anger soared. Fat Mama walked right up to him and slapped the shit out of him with her toolie.

"What—the—fuck—bitch," he stuttered as she beat him relentlessly. She knew he was a killer, but at that moment, she didn't give two fucks. She felt hands trying to pry her off his dirty-ass body. It was her cousin.

"Please, get off him," Susie screamed.

"Bitch, get yo' hands off me! You gon' defend this nigga?" Fat Mama knocked her hands away, screaming in her face. "Fuck you. I hope he kills yo' dumb ass."

As she turned to leave, she spotted a .357 sitting on a wooden table. Beside it were two kilos of heroin. The first thing she thought about was her brothers. Judah would know what to do with it. He was street to the fullest and already knew how to whip, thanks to her. She'd picked up a few things from her BD and the streets.

She snatched the kilos and stuffed them into her purse.

"Hold up, cousin. You not about to take that," Susie spat, acting like she wanted smoke.

"Bitch, I'll blow yo' head off if you take another step."

"Damn, you gon' steal from yo' own family?"

"Bitch, we ain't shit. In my eyes, you died the day you started using drugs. You a washed-up, crackhead-ass hoe," Fat Mama spat in her face and made her exit.

On her way out, she heard Shoota Face growl, "The bitch should've killed me. On everything, I won't spare her life."

Fat Mama was startled out of her reverie by her son. He hugged her legs, rocking back and forth. "I love you. I love you."

She picked him up and kissed him. "I love you, too."

"If you did, bitch, why the fuck did you suck the opp's dick?"

She almost dropped her son when his face and voice morphed into his father's.

"Mama, did you hear me? I said I love you more and more and more."

Right then, a sudden wave of regret washed over her like a flood. She still couldn't believe she'd put Hideous's dick in her mouth, but she'd wanted to kill him that bad. She knew she had to get her mind off him before the fire consumed her. She focused back on the money.

Chapter 17

No Escape

A week after getting Lil' T's number at the club, Fat Mama was seeing him every day since. He was spoiling her with all the things she could ever wish for. She was a bad bitch. He hadn't even got the pussy yet. She teased him a lot though. She knew if she was going to kidnap him for half a million dollars, she had to make it look like it wasn't on her. Niggas on his father's level in the game weren't stupid. Suddenly, when she started fucking with him, he gets kidnapped. Naw she had a plan.

She knew all about his beef with a nigga named K9. Lil' T dropped some dick off in his BM and exposed her on social media. The beef turned to war. So bad Big T got involved, killing a handful of K9's people. And they robbed a lot of his spots, but one, and Fat Mama had it all covered.

Cain parked in front of K9's trap, and the three of them got out of the car. He knew Fat Mama was going to bitch about them bringing her precious Mark. She didn't want him doing anything his older brothers were doing; she wanted him to stay away from that side of the life, but she knew he had a few bodies on his resume.

The trap was illuminated with a lot of light, but Cain didn't give a fuck. K9's niggas better be strapped. They crept around back; it didn't take Cain much to kick the back door off its hinges.

Paul gripped the Draco as his older brother kicked down the door. All three brothers ran inside, awaiting death to show its naked face.

Two thick hoes were naked, twerking to some *Zeethewizard* thumping from the surround sound speakers, while three niggas sat watching nothing but ass and titties bounce like a state fair ride. K9 was one of the niggas. They tried to make a move but were instantly turned into paper targets.

Budda-Budda-Budda-Budda.

Cain and Paul did damage to the three niggas, tearing their flesh and bodies into a bloody mess. Their upper bodies did the shoulder lean while their bottoms did the running man. The two thick hoes' bodies were dismantled and sprawled out on the bloody carpet.

Cain walked over with the Draco braced against his chest. He looked to Mark and nodded toward the back rooms.

Mark proceeded through the shotgun-shaped house, down the hall, toting a Draco. His heel smashed through the door and watched it bust open. As he went inside, he looked all through the room with his Draco ready to make a fuck nigga breakdance, but instead, he came across a duffle bag and two guns. A Glock 17 and a Beretta 92.

Back in the living room, Cain was snapping pictures of K9's dead corpse when Mark returned, handing him the Goyard bag filled with money. Cain opened it, and it had thousands of small glassine packets full of dirty brown powder. Heroin, cut and cut again, packaged and ready to be sold.

Mark gave the two guns to Paul, and Paul displayed all 32s. Paul loved guns, and he was gonna add those two beauties to his collection.

When they made it outside, a couple of people had heard the gunshots. Some sat on the sidewalk, some in the yard. Three of them were women; the rest were hard-looking niggas.

The brothers didn't give a fuck. They waved their Dracos in all directions until they made it back to the getaway car.

Cain got behind the wheel, Paul got in the back, and Mark in the passenger seat. Before they sped away, Cain said, "Throw some of that money out the window." He knew his older brother would've done just that to attract attention off of them.

"What?" Paul said from the back.

"You heard what the fuck I said," Cain shot back.

Paul was far from a hoe, but the one person he knew he had no win with was his older brother Cain. The nigga was massive. He'd been hit by him once and thought the nigga broke his jaw. Paul reached into the bag, popped a rubber band full of money, and threw it out the window as the car sped away. Money blew everywhere. People ran into the road, scoping it up. The same hard-looking niggas turned into groupies. Cain busted a hard right at the end of the diagonal street, and after that, Hatcher Street was lost in sight.

Later That Afternoon…

Fat Mama was sitting on her bed, getting ready to meet with Lil' T to spend the weekend with him at his apartment in North Dallas. A few feet away, her son stood in the doorway of her room; he had a smile on his face. She gave him everything he wanted. He watched his T-Jones put makeup on her face. He loved her so much.

"Mama, why do you wear that? You look pretty without it," he said, still smiling.

She looked up and was about to say something when her three brothers entered her room with a Goyard bag. She was mad at first because they took Mark. They knew he was off-limits. Her frown turned into a smile when Cain stepped up with his iPhone in her face. All she saw were three bloody bodies, one being K9. He zoomed in a little. K9's body was like a pretzel. His neck was twisted at an impossible angle.

He had to die for Big T to believe K9's people had something to do with the kidnapping.

She looked over at Paul as the bag in his hand fell open, and an avalanche of money came pouring onto the bed.

She swore, looking at that money, it got her pussy super wet. Mark sat on the bed, checking the guns with Paul. They were both loaded, with one in the chamber.

Fat Mama turned her attention to the money and picked up a bunch of it. She knew more money was ‘bout to come after the kidnapping. First, she had to get with him.

Chapter 18

The Kidnapping of a Hustler's Son

The millionaire drug dealer, Big T, admired his Instagram-model-looking bitch as she came down the stairs naked in his luxurious townhome with her ass claps echoing softly against the wood, her outrageous booty jiggling with every move she made. Her name was Ike, and she was known across the city as one of the baddest. She'd been in numerous magazines; her latest was *Kite DM*. She carried herself like the queen of the underworld she was, her melon-sized tits bouncing in sync with a walk that was worth more than most niggas' stash houses. She was a mix of Cuban and White but had a coffee-colored complexion.

Ike worked on her body on the daily—toning, tanning, and losing any excess fat. She adored her humongous ass; it was the size of Gracie Bon's. Her ass had brought in so much more money since it'd been added to her everyday life. Ass shots were the trend, and she'd gotten hers off a dope boy.

"Damn, you smell so damn good," Big T said, wrapping his arms around her from behind. She felt his exposed erection against her soft ass.

"Not now, bae," she said, wriggling out of his grasp.

He looked at his bustdown Rollie and said, "I wonder why my lil' nigga ain't called me all day."

"Where he at?" Ike asked.

He grabbed her hand and pulled her to him. He pushed her down to her knees. "Baby, hold up," she moaned. She glanced up; his dick was hard and vibrating like a knife thrown into a wooden door. She kissed it like it had never been kissed before. Then, with one smooth motion, she took half the dick into her mouth.

Soon his face twisted as she worked. He arched his back, his muscles coiling tight like a spring about to snap, loving the way her throat gripped him. Her mouth was just as hot and wet as her pussy. She would swallow his dick with one movement, letting it slide all the way to the back of her throat. Then, at the moment of deepest penetration, she would lick at his balls with her tongue while simultaneously sucking his dick down her throat. The feeling was intense—so intense that he grunted, his whole body vibrating as he shot what was probably the biggest nut of his life straight into her mouth. She swallowed every last drop.

Lil' T's Apartment…

Lil T was lying across the bed staring at his iPhone when soft knocks on the door startled him. He stood up and walked to the door, dick already rocked up. When he looked through the peephole, he saw Fat Mama standing there waiting.

He opened the door and Fat Mama walked in. She wore black Skims leggings tighter than a ballerina's fit, and a small halter top. For the last week, she'd been weaving Lil' T into her web. She'd even cooked for him, but she'd never given him any ass.

But he was feeling himself today.

He locked the front door, walked over, and smacked Fat Mama's chunky ass as she did a slow 360, taking the room in. He loved the way it jiggled. He wrapped his arms around her waist from behind and led her to his bedroom, his gaze glued to her backside. He watched as that big booty jiggled like a set of keys.

"I see somebody's happy to see me." She reached back and grabbed his dick through his Gucci briefs.

Within seconds, his hands found her leggings and stripped them from her thick body. “Hold up, nigga.” She turned around and stuck her ass right in his face. “Eat my ass.” She spread it open with both hands, showing him her crinkled skin. She ran her fingertip over it, causing it to gape. She reached back, grabbed his bald head, and smashed his face into her. He stuck out his tongue as far as it could go, rimming her as she humped his face, making little moaning sounds.

“Okay, nigga. Okay.” She grabbed the back of his head and began grinding her big ass as hard as she could into his face. Just as he thought he was going to suffocate, her body began to vibrate and she gasped as she came, gushing pussy juice onto his face.

She spread her cheeks over the tip of his tongue and sank down, taking it deep. Then she began riding his face up and down, fucking herself with his stiff tongue.

He sho’ thanked them *Phat Puff* magazines he’d read daily when he was locked up for those two years. Every article from Issue 1 to 12 popped into his head. His favorite was Issue 9; he loved Thugga Doll. She was so sexy to him. He remembered her saying to use a lot of tongue, which he was doing right then and there.

Finally, Lil’ T stood up and shed his briefs. His dick was level with Fat Mama’s mouth. She leaned over and smelled it before she started sucking it like she was possessed. He couldn’t help but notice her big ass sticking out like the side of a couch. He had to get a sample. He led her over to the dry bar on one side of his living room. He pulled out one of the stools and told her to sit.

“Fuck me good, nigga.” She leaned forward, sticking her ass out. She reached back, grabbed his balls, and pulled him in. He aimed his dick toward her. He took some lube in his hand, rubbed it on the head of his dick, then slowly inserted himself. She was incredibly tight and even hotter than her pussy. She grunted as he gradually sank in up to his balls.

"That's it, baby . . . fuck my ass," she groaned as he stroked in and out. He grabbed her waist and began hitting it as hard as he could, his body slapping against her big, jiggly cheeks.

Wham-Wham-Wham.

Even though Lil' T was handling his business, the only thing on Fat Mama's mind was money. In a couple of hours, he was going to be beaten and tossed into the back of a stolen van. She knew his old man had already received the picture she sent of K9. While Big T was at war trying to kill the rest of K9's flunkies, Fat Mama and her brothers would be long gone before anyone realized she was the one behind the abduction.

Outside the luxury apartment, the windowless box truck sat in front of Lil' T's building. Paul stroked the trigger of the Draco as he grew tired of waiting for his sister's further instructions. The brothers cast furtive glances at one another. The uncertainty of what they were about to face filled them with trepidation. Lil' T's old man was a drug kingpin, but kingpins died, too.

"Ugh, she needs to hurry the fuck up," Milky Way whined. She was a gutta bitch trapped in a geek-bitch body—like a Black version of Velma from *Scooby-Doo*, tortoise-shell glasses and all. But she was far from a geek; she was a gangsta-ass bitch with an ass like Tommie Lee.

"Bitch, shut up and get dressed. You're up," Cain barked.

She rolled her eyes. "I bet if Judah was here, you wouldn't talk that hot shit."

"I bet I would," he shot back while the others laughed.

Mark and Paul got quiet as church mice, watching Milky Way peel off her clothes in the back of the van. Her pussy was fat and shaved bald, her titties round, and her ass almost too heavy to carry. She slipped on the maid outfit the building required for employees. She realized she held their attention and snapped, "Close y'all muthafuckin' mouths, acting like y'all never seen no coochie before. Y'all ain't shit but a bunch of perverts."

Mark took a deep breath. Even though his sister and her friends were strippers, he always had a hard time being around Milky Way. She had that dangerous sex appeal. He hoped one day to be in his brother's shoes—Judah was fucking all his sister's homegirls, including Milky Way.

She hopped out of the van and stepped onto the street. Cain was still parked near the curb a hundred yards away. She texted him to hit the block because the van looked suspicious as fuck in that upscale neighborhood. He drove twenty yards down, busted a U-turn, and came back slowly, easing to a stop just out of sight.

They opened the doors and climbed out, pulling plastic masks over their faces. It was important Lil' T didn't see them. There was no easy way to hide a Draco, so Cain carried it down by his leg.

The play was to wait in the stairwell. Milky Way opened the side door and led them up four flights. For a million dollars, she'd run up twenty flights butt-naked. Cain watched as she held the door open—the entry point to a half-million-dollar payday. The three brothers stayed put, waiting for the next play.

A Moment Later…

When a knock came from the door, followed by a couple more hard knocks, Lil T jumped straight up in the bed with a confused look on his face.

Fat Mama lay naked beside him, still asleep—or so he thought. He looked at his bustdown Rolex and saw it was 9:41 in the morning. *Who the fuck is this?* he thought. But before he could think on it, Fat Mama said, "Bae, get the door. I ordered some room service."

"Room service?" he mumbled, easing up from the bed and pushing Fat Mama to the side. He didn't even know a place like this had room service, but then again, it was connected to a hotel. His feet came into contact with the plush carpet as the person behind the door continued to hit it with strong knocks.

Bang. Bang. Bang.

Looking through the peephole, a sense of relief washed over him. He saw that it was only an attractive, thick, college-professor-looking maid standing outside wearing some cute glasses. She was standing by a pushcart with a silver tray on top—the kind you usually see in movies. He was from the PJs; he wasn't used to no shit like that.

He opened the door and let the sexy maid inside. When she passed him pushing the cart, all he saw was ass. "Damn!" he mumbled, not believing the weight that sat on this maid's back.

His eyes widened even larger when she reached for the tray, picked up a Glock 17, and pointed it at him. "What the fuck," he screamed, just as he was knocked to the floor with the butt of the gun.

"What the fuck is going on in here?" Fat Mama looked up, startled, as Milky Way stood over Lil' T with the Glock. He was petrified.

Fat Mama's scream was cut short as Milky Way pressed the gun to her forehead. "Bitch, shut the fuck up before I blow yo' top halfway across this muthafucka."

At that moment, three masked gunmen rushed in, all toting assault rifles. Lil' T looked numb, fear in his eyes and unable to speak. He stared, terrified, at Fat Mama. She pleaded with him with her eyes.

Three Days Later…

"*Mmmgh-hmp*," Lil' T's muffled scream strained against the gag. Every breath was a struggle against the damp fabric stuffed in his mouth. He lay on the freezing concrete, cuffed and blindfolded, lost in a suffocating darkness where time had no meaning. The space was a tomb, squeezing the life out of him. Then the heavy tumblers of a lock turned. The door groaned open, spilling a draft of ice-cold air over his trembling frame. The gag was snatched out, nearly taking his teeth with it, and the blindfold was ripped free, leaving him blinking and broken in the sudden harsh light.

Damn, where are all my clothes? Why would they strip me naked? The scenarios in his head were gruesome and horrific—straight slaughterhouse. He felt the cold concrete floor pressing against every inch of his bare skin, making him feel smaller than he'd ever been in his life. He was a millionaire's son, but right now, he was just a piece of meat waiting for the blade.

Lil' T jumped violently when Milky Way came in and softly caressed his right cheek with the stainless-steel machete. She squatted right in his face. His scared eyes were literally staring at her phat mound through the black Skims bodysuit she now wore.

"Now, I'm going to ask you some'," she said as she jabbed him with the butt of the machete. "Your father agreed to pay the five-hundred-thousand-dollar ransom for you, but who is the bitch with you?"

"My—bitch—please—don't—hurt—her," he stuttered over his words.

At that moment, two masked gunmen threw Fat Mama's half-naked ass into the small room. Milky Way looked at her with disgust. "This the bitch you dyin' behind? With that, Milky Way stood up and followed the two gunmen out the door.

"Fat Mama—Fat Mama," Lil' T whispered once the door was closed shut.

"I'm scared, daddy. They are talking about killing us."

"My father is on his way to pay for our ransom."

Chapter 19

Pay Or Die

A ten-stack of hundreds made ten thousand dollars per brick. There was a mountain of cash sitting in front of Big T, stacked high and tight.

Ike asked, "How much is that?"

"More than two hundred racks," he said.

"How much more do you need?"

"Three hundred more."

It was quiet for a very long time. Then she said, "What we waiting for?"

"The rest of the money."

Within seconds, one of his men came in toting a large duffel bag filled with the rest of the ransom money. "Here goes three hundred thousand like you requested, boss," X said as he dropped the money to the floor. "What you want me to do now?"

"Stay put and wait for my call. They want me to come alone."

Later…

The field in Lancaster ran unbroken for more than ten straight miles. The dirt road turned east at its far corner, then west again, all the way to the pickup point. The road narrowed back to a farmyard where a large shelter stood in the background. Up ahead was a black van. Standing on the side of it were two masked gunmen toting a Draco with a drum that was thicker than a Snickers.

Milky Way rocked a ski mask as well, her eyes cold as she pressed the muzzle of her gun into Lil' T's temple. He was a trembling mess, a black pillowcase draped over his head like a funeral shroud. Right beside him, Fat Mama played her part to perfection—stripped down and forced onto her knees on the jagged gravel, her own head hooded as she waited for the "death" she'd already choreographed.

"What the fuck my boy done got himself into?" Big T said out loud. He had gotten the picture of three dead muthafuckas—one being his son's enemy—with a message attached that read:

We know you and your son had sum' to do with our nigga being killed. It's okay, we got his pussy ass and you gon' pay to get him back, or he gon' end up like K9.

After making a lot of sacrifices and empty promises, here he was in the middle of nowhere, all alone with nothing but half a million dollars. He parked the Bentley near the large shelter, just outside a fence that was six times his size.

The two masked gunmen stood shoulder to shoulder, one on each side of his son. Big T got out of the Bentley dressed in Versace from head to toe, carrying a Louis Vuitton bag in his hand.

Milky Way nodded at Cain, and he went and grabbed the bag. Cain checked the contents, flipping through the dead presidents. He nodded, and Milky Way pushed Lil' T forward. When he made it to his pops, they hopped into the car.

Inside, Big T yanked the pillowcase from his son's head.

"Noooo! We can't leave her!" Lil' T screamed at his father, but it was like talking to a wall. He watched as the two masked gunmen led Fat Mama back into the shelter.

Budda-Budda-Budda. Gunfire filled the air.

"Noooo," he screamed, his hands still tied behind his back. He couldn't believe he'd gotten Fat Mama killed. He just stared at the shelter, numb, confused, and angry.

Fat Mama sat on the sofa watching her brothers count out half a million dollars. Over the last week, she'd planned the perfect heist, and it had worked to her advantage. She'd just pulled off a big score by finessing a nigga with some ass.

Her phone vibrated. She looked at the message now staring at her. It was from Hideous.

What it do? When can a nigga see you? I hope you remember a nigga. I'm the ugly nigga from the club.

He sent another picture that almost made her vomit—a shot of his dick in his hand. She knew one thing: she was going to kill him, even if it meant putting that pussy on him one last time.

Because as a nigga can see, her pussy was deadly.

Chapter 20

Chemical Hearts

Sabrina was a beautiful young woman who knew how to use her beauty to her advantage. She had been over at Hideous's spot for over a week and had learned everything there was to know about Uzi Mi. Hideous wanted to hit his main stash spot out in Cedar Hill. Even though Uzi Mi was living the good life in Miami, he kept all the money he made in Texas at his spot in Cedar Hill.

Sabrina warned Hideous that it was heavily guarded, but Hideous didn't give two fucks. He wanted to make Uzi Mi suffer. Until he sold the diamonds to go to war with him, he was going to fuck up everything he had going on in Texas.

The only problem was the two bitches she'd gotten cool with to get intel on Uzi Mi were two dyke hoes who kept trying to get inside her panties. She wasn't into bitches at all, but they were her only way inside Uzi Mi's operation.

Sabrina wore a cut-off T-shirt that exposed the bottoms of her large tits, playing it for all it was worth. She gasped quietly when she felt one of the dykes finally made a move, feeling those fingers trail up her leg and hook deep into her boyshorts, claiming territory against her skin. She looked at the other one, who had lust written all over her face. Sabrina slept sandwiched between the two. Indii was on her side with her hand inside Sabrina's shorts, while Macy had one or two fingers in Sabrina's pussy as well. After a series of soft, slow moans, Sabrina arched her back, rolling onto her side to face Macy while grinding her ass against Indii.

Macy pulled Sabrina's shirt up, burying her face in her 46-inch Double-Ds, devouring them while Indii's hand played deep inside her boyshorts. The fabric didn't stay long; Macy reached down and stripped the boyshorts past Sabrina's knees, leaving her completely exposed. Indii's hand quickly returned, her fingers exploring and finding Sabrina's pussy soaking wet. She moaned deeply.

Sabrina looked at Macy with half-closed eyes, twisting her body and squirming her juicy ass against Indii as Macy's mouth moved from her breasts to her throat, sucking hard enough to leave a mark. Sabrina shifted her weight, rolling to face Indii so she could return the favor, her hands reaching out to massage and knead Indii's heat. But as she focused on the front, she left her ass wide open. Macy didn't waste the opportunity.

From behind, Macy hooked a firm hand under Sabrina's top leg, hoisting it toward the ceiling and spreading her wide open. Before Sabrina could even process the vulnerability, she felt something big slide into her. There was no hesitation; the solid, synthetic head of the dildo breached her, sliding in with a slick, heavy friction that claimed every inch of her pussy.

Sabrina's eyes didn't just open— they nearly popped out of her head as her spine arched into a rigid bow. A long, shattered moan tore from her throat, vibrating through the room.

"*Oh my gawd.*"

She buckled under the weight of the invasion, her bodybody instinctively pushing back to accept the twelve-inch strap-on Macy now wore around her waist. The massive purple dildo invaded Sabrina's pussy wall, going deeper than any real dick had ever gone before. Macy rolled over between her legs, spreading them wide so she could take even more. Her movements were harder now, more forceful.

Sabrina was moaning and panting hard, her large tits bouncing and shuddering with each stroke.

When Hideous stepped inside Sabrina's crib, he was smoking a Newport cigarette. He exhaled twin streams of white smoke through his nostrils. Hearing moaning coming from the bedroom, he walked in on a straight porno in the making.

Indii was so horny that she hopped up, shoved him against the wall, and stuck her hand down his pants. "Who this nigga is, Sabrina? He yo' man or some shit?" she spat, stroking his dick to its full potential. "You wouldn't mind if we fuck him?"

"You want this dick, huh?" He roughly threw her around so her back was facing him. "Put 'cha hands up against the wall!" She did as instructed. He smacked both of her ass cheeks. "Toot this shit up and spread these fucking legs." He kicked her legs apart like he was the popo doing a strip search.

Hideous bit his bottom lip as he watched his dick disappear and reappear. Indii's pussy had his dick creamy as fuck, like it was dipped in some whipped cream. He continued to fuck her with all his might—hard and deep. Her ass jiggled all over the place; he watched the ripple effect through her cheeks with each hard stroke. He gripped her soft ass and buried his thumb in her tight opening. He started rubbing her, and before he knew it, Indii started throwing it back on him. Her back was arched and her ass was tooted, throwing it everywhere.

Hideous watched her work his twelve-inch dick.

On the bed, Macy was stroking the dildo as hard as she could muster inside Sabrina's tight, sloppy pussy. "Oh, my gawd," Sabrina moaned as Macy thrust mercilessly. She grabbed onto one of her own enormous titties, squeezing it for support as her body was rocked forward with every heavy thrust. Her eyes rolled back in her head, her breath coming in ragged, shallow hitches until her body finally gave out.

She collapsed into the pillows, a quivering, soaking-wet mess, her legs still twitching from the vibration of the dildo. But the heat in the room didn't cool down; it just changed targets.

Macy unbuckled the harness, letting the purple monster clatter to the floor as her eyes locked onto the show by the wall.

Meanwhile, Hideous grabbed Indii by the waist and started to pound her as hard as he could. Her ass just continued to bounce. All he could think about was Jell-O. Macy was mesmerized by the sight of Indii's ass slapping back against Hideous's nutsack with a rhythmic, wet thud. It was hypnotic—the way the flesh jiggled from side to side like it was waving a flag of surrender. The way her ass bounced back from every soul-snatching stroke played like a Bunz 4 Ever porno stuck on a high-speed repeat.

Unable to stay on the sidelines, Macy scrambled off the bed and stood behind Hideous. She wrapped her arms around his waist, her hands adding to the momentum as she helped push and pull Indii's ass back and forth against him. She was guiding the collision, making sure every stroke went as deep as possible.

From the bed, Sabrina watched through a haze of exhaustion as the two dykes went ham. They weren't just fucking; they were acting like they'd been starving for the D for a very long time and Hideous was the only meal in town.

The air in the room was thick enough to choke on. One by one, they migrated to the king-sized bed, converging on the silk sheets where Sabrina lay flushed and gasping. Hideous climbed onto the mattress, leaning his back against the headboard like a king on the throne, while the two dykes swarmed around him. Then Hideous resumed fucking Indii.

After Indii had *come* for the hundredth time, her body finally went limp, but the hunger in the room was still starving. Macy didn't waste a second; she scrambled into the centre of the matress and got into a low squat position right in front of Hideous. She reached back with both hands, grabbing her own butt cheeks and busting that shit wide open for the world to see.

Indii rolled off the bed just long enough to snatch the discarded strap-on dildo from the floor. She stepped into the leather loops and cinched the harness tight around her slim waist. The twelve-inch monster jerked upward as the buckle clicked, locking it into place as she climbed back onto the bed behind Macy.

But Macy wasn't waiting for the dildo. She had her eyes on a different prize.

She lunged at Hideous, sucking his dick like she was bobbing for a gold apple. She picked up speed, and her head was moving with the rhythmic precision of a power drill—fast, steady, relentless. She was a straight **Headhunter**, sucking and slurping with such ferocity that saliva began to leak from the corners of her mouth and trail down her chin. In that moment, she could admit it to herself: she'd missed sucking dick.

Hideous sat back against the headboard, his breath hitching as he watched his dick disappear and reappear in the vacuum of Macy's mouth. He reached down, threading his fingers through her hair and gripping the back of her head to guide her rhythm. He started feeding it to her, pushing deeper and deeper until her throat constricted and she started gagging. She was deep-throating him like her life depended on it, her eyes watering as she took up the challenge. She was taking so much dick in her mouth, she had to pull away to spit some glob of saliva onto the floor. She took a deep, ragged breath and dived back in, her mouth making slurping sounds on his dick. Even with her throat stretched to the limit, he was still only halfway in.

Uck-Uck-Uck. The sound was wet, raw, choked—the unmistakable noise of a woman filled past her capacity. She was gagging on the thickness, her lungs burning for air, but she didn't pull back. She just gripped his thighs and leaned into the stretch, determined to swallow every bit of the work he was feeding her.

10 Minutes Later…

While Indii was still coming off the high of Hideous's 12-inch dick, she moved into position rocking that purple 12-inch strap-on. It was pumped up like Barney around her waist, and she was moving with the confidence of an adult porn legend like Pinky. She slowly pushed the head of the dildo into Macy's small, tight asshole. Macy wanted to cry as she got double-penetrated to the point all she could do was *come* back-to-back until she felt like throwing in the towel.

"Hell naw. Hell naw. Fuck!" Macy screamed, her body fighting to take twenty-four inches of work inside her all at once.

Hideous eventually turned his attention to Sabrina. She lay on the bed with her legs spread wide, staring at his dick like she was under a spell. He motioned for her to come to him, and she crawled over without hesitation. She looked up at him, breathless, and said, "It's so big." She kissed the head and licked the entire length of the shaft, opening her mouth wide, only to realize she could only get half of it down her throat.

A few moments later, Hideous told her to suck him faster and to open her mouth wider. He then erupted, shooting stream after stream of thick white cum into her mouth and onto her big tits.

"Damn!" Sabrina said, amazed at the sheer volume of the cum. She laid back between Macy's open legs, but Hideous wasn't done yet—he wanted one of them to suck him dry, so he positioned himself on one side of Macy's face while Indii, still strapped up, was on the other side.

Sabrina began to finger herself, watching as Macy licked and sucked on both the real dick and the dildo, moving from one to the other and back again in a feverish rhythm. Macy looked up, her eyes glazed with lust. "I love tasting my pussy and ass on y'all dick. I miss dick so much. It gives me a rush."

Hideous just leaned back and watched Macy eat. For a hustla, dreams were made of moments like this.

Chapter 21

Fuck Uzi Mi

The next morning, Sabrina was lying flat on top of Hideous, her soft, heavy tits pressed against his chest. He was gripping two chunky ass cheeks, his dick getting harder with every squeeze. He knew he had to get back to business; Sabrina had given up the location of Uzi Mi's main stash house, thanks to Indii and Macy. He planned on checking things out immediately. He wanted Uzi Mi to know shit was about to get real.

"I want to really thank you for not playing me and my bitches. I really appreciate you," Sabrina said. She was from the projects; nobody ever gave a fuck about her. But Hideous kept it 100 while everybody she'd ever trusted tried to play on her top. There weren't many real niggas moving like Hideous. He was a meal ticket, and she loved how he spoiled her with attention. She was just grateful to be getting some real money without having to get naked or lay on her back for it.

She started to make her ass jump in his hand while she played with his ear with her tongue. "Your sister looks exactly like one of Macy's homegirls back in Miami. They dealing with Uzi Mi's uncle directly. They work for him, and they're loyal to him."

"Oh yeah? I'm gon' meet them real soon as well. Then I'm putting a bullet in their heads, too."

"Damn, y'all still in the bed fucking?" Macy asked as she stepped into the room, dressed and ready to hit the streets.

A couple of hours later in Cedar Hill, Hideous dragged the back of his sleeve across his eyes, squinting into the sun as he stepped out of the stolen Tesla with his girls—Butt-Butt and Bunz. He'd thanked Sabrina for getting him this far, but it was time for work. He scanned the unknown area, looking for movement.

As Butt-Butt and Bunz made it to the front of the Tesla, a single shot rang out. A fraction of a second later, the bullet slapped into Bunz's neck, spinning her around and dropping her to the ground in a pool of her own blood. She reached up and clamped at her throat, not believing she had just been hit.

What the fuck just happened? Hideous thought. He immediately took cover behind the Tesla with Butt-Butt at his side. She was lost for words, staring at her best friend.

"Stay down!" he shouted.

"You came to the wrong spot, bitch!" a voice called from a crumbled-up house nearby.

An immediate hail of bullets rocked the Tesla.

Budda-Budda-Budda.

When the shooting ceased, Hideous craned his head up to see over the top of the vehicle. Another bullet thudded heavily into the metal, and he dropped back down. "It's two, maybe more. I know for sho' there's two shooting at us," Hideous said, looking at a frightened Butt-Butt. She was shaking harder than she ever did on a stripper pole.

Hideous stretched out his arm, pushed his Uzi over the top of the Tesla, and sprayed in the direction of the house. "Stay here and don't move. Shoot when I tell you. I got this. I promise."

A quick succession of shots rang out as he burst from the side of the shattered Tesla, Uzi in hand, sliding toward a Benz parked in the driveway.

"Shoot now!" Hideous shouted.

Butt-Butt groaned as she stood up, rested her arms on the roof of the Tesla, and aimed her Glock 17. She fired off a couple of shots. There was movement in the doorway Hideous was aiming at, and he squeezed the trigger, his shots peppering the walls and windows.

Butt-Butt was about to lower her gun when sunlight glinted on the barrel of a weapon appearing in the window. Hideous rose to one knee, then stood completely up just as Butt-Butt's Glock went the fuck off, dropping a nigga in the open window.

Hideous made his move.

He took off running toward the house, half-stumbled, and fell over the entrance step. He leaned against the wall after stepping over the nigga toting the Draco. He kept his Uzi as steady as he could, knowing the other shooter had run upstairs right after his partner got cut down.

That was where the real danger lay. A trickle of sweat ran from his forehead and into his eye. He dragged the sleeve of his black hoodie across his face again. He looked around the house; the furniture was riddled with bullet holes.

Moving forward, he kept his Uzi raised at shoulder level. He climbed each step slowly, leaning against the right-hand wall to make himself a smaller target. He was on the sixth step, a third of the way up, when a dyke bitch raised her gun. Before she could fire, a high-velocity bullet punched through her forehead, knocking her off her feet.

It was Macy. The bitch he'd fucked just last night. It was an ambush; she must've overheard him and Sabrina talking.

The sound of the shot still rang deafeningly as her body slid down the wall. The other nigga took a step toward his cousin before a spray of bullets from the Uzi tore him down like a demolition ball hitting a building. He crashed to his knees, not knowing Hideous was that close. His body tumbled sideways, dead before he hit the ground.

When Hideous made it to the upper level, he checked each room, praying to empty the clip into more flesh.

Coming up short, he headed back, stepping over Macy and her cousin. He sprayed them both as they lay on the floor, tagging them like they were graffiti.

Back downstairs, Butt-Butt had dragged Bunz's body into the house. She was kneeling over her, crying hysterically. "Not my bitch, Hideous. Look at what they've done."

After a long sigh, Hideous looked at the hurt in her eyes. He thought about the same pain he felt when his sister had died in his arms.

"Babygirl, I know it hurt, but we got to go. We got to finish what Uzi Mi started. We got to kill his ass for the pain he caused us."

"Fuck Uzi Mi!" she screamed. For a brief second, Hideous didn't know if he was going to have to turn his gun on her.

"Use that hate to kill yo' enemies," was his only advice.

Butt-Butt looked across at him and broke a smile. *Fuck Uzi Mi. I'm going kill him and piss on his coffin.*

Two Hours Later…

Flip had been driving all around the city, picking up money, at the time his trap was getting hit for nine bricks and close to $63,000. He knew Uzi Mi was going to be devastated when he heard the news.

First Flyboi, and now Black. He headed to his safe house in the cliff where he had his bitch and two kids ducked off, patiently waiting to go to the state fair. But he knew he had to call Uzi Mi first.

Chapter 22

Miami Baby

Uzi Mi's suite sat on a beautiful scenery in the back of his uncle's $1.2 million dollar mansion, offering a view of some of the most beautiful scenery in the city. It was a palace built on blood and bricks; all thanks to Hideous, who had contributed heavily to his uncle's investments. Uzi Mi stood by the floor-to-ceiling glass, staring at a crystal-clear ocean that stretched miles and miles beyond the horizon.

Miami was truly beautiful.

He sat back, the smooth sounds of Zillionaire Doe echoing somewhere deep in the large house. His heart still ached from the loss of Rachel. She was a beautiful soul and died too soon before her life even started. He knew one day Hideous would come for him with guns blazing, but he'd be ready. His uncle owned Miami, and he had an army of crazy Haitians who were ready to die for the cause.

Uzi Mi's face tensed into a mask of pure, strained pleasure every time Jelly deep-throated his dick in her mouth. He watched with hooded eyes as his dick went in and out of her pretty mouth. In and out. In and out. She licked at his balls, then stuffed the dick back down her throat. She began slowly engulfing it while licking the side of it like it was a popsicle. She would swallow his dick with one movement, letting it slide all the way to the back of her throat.

"You ready for all this, baby?" Jelly asked, standing to her feet after sucking his dick dry. For over a month, she had been working out; her body was toned and firm, sporting a six-pack and everything. Her body was on point. Her ass was chunky as hell—so much so that she could rival Moneybagg's hoe, Ari.

The only thing in Uzi Mi's vision was a well-shaved pussy. Jelly straddled his lap, facing him so that he was looking at the large tits he'd paid for. She slowly impaled herself on his dick, eventually taking the entire thing in. He stretched her wider and filled her deeper than her last nigga ever could. Once she had his dick all the way in, she began bouncing up and down on his lap. As her ass started clapping nonstop, he went after those tits, licking and sucking them voraciously. Her hips took on a life of their own, and she began to bounce even more wildly than before, bringing herself to a second climax.

He was enjoying the feel of his bitch's fat, rounded ass under his hands when the shrill hip-hop ringtone of his iPhone bounced off the walls. He fumbled to grab the smartphone, but Jelly got to it first. She didn't even bother to look at the screen; she just tossed it behind her. She looked deep into his eyes and rode that dick even harder.

Finally, the ringing stopped, but when Uzi Mi did get to his phone, he regretted it. He was angrier at himself than he was at Jelly. He'd let his guard down, acting weak for that lil' pussy, and now he had to pay the price for being distracted. The conversation he just had with Flip was one he wished he hadn't. He'd known Hideous was gon' come for him eventually, but damn—the nigga had come hard. Hideous hadn't just hit the trap; he'd killed two of Uzi Mi's main hitters. Flip and Black.

He was tripping, but not just about Hideous gunning for him. The stakes had tripled; his uncle was currently locked in a brutal turf war with the Jamaicans, who were claiming territory block by block. The Jamaicans were growing many new followers each day. They were deadly and unpredictable. And they wanted Uzi Mi's uncle dead with the rest of his team.

Thirty bodies were already scattered all over the beautiful city of Miami, victims from both sides of the field. It was gruesome. The city was bleeding, and soon someone was going to claim the throne: either the Haitians or the Jamaicans.

Uzi Mi dug between the the cushions of the sofa, his fingers grazing leather until he found what he was searching for: a Tec-9 with an extended clip already locked in.

"Where you going?" Jelly asked, naked on the Peloton, her voluptuous body glistening with sweat under the sunlight beaming through the enormous windows.

"To end one beef and prepare for another, because I know Hideous will be here at any given time. And these Young Peckham Boyz are becoming a serious problem."

"Be careful. The YPB niggas are laying shit down," she warned, staring into the screen at the instructor that was guiding her through an intense workout.

Uzi Mi took one last look at Jelly's ass as it jiggled with every pedal stroke. He knew one thing for certain: his enemies were going to die before they could kill him.

Later…

Ada and Lucia lounged in their glass-walled luxury apartment, casually sipping on flutes of vintage champagne. They were both naked as the day they were born into the world, their skin glowing under the recessed lighting. Lucia was a Cuban bitch that looked good enough to eat. She had a smooth, coconut-cream complexion with an ass as fat as a pregnant donkey.Ada, on the other hand, was that Latto-colored, honey-gold skin. She was from South Africa. She had so much ass it felt like she could feed her entire village in Cape Town. She was stacked with the kind of legendary curves and ass that would make Zmeena Orr look twice, her hips flaring out into a shelf that defied gravity.

They sat there sipping Don Julio straight out of the bottle, waiting for the man of the hour. Ada looked up at the state-of-the-art LED television screen and saw Uzi Mi approaching on the security feed. Lucia smiled at him as he stepped inside the house, using his own key to gain entry.

He got straight to business. "Did y'all handle that issue? I heard Leroy and Delroy were at Klub 24 Miami the other night."

"Naw, we didn't," Ada said, standing up to pour Uzi Mi a glass of champagne. Like most men, Uzi Mi's eyes were glued to her gigantic ass.

"How is y'all not able to entice a bunch of eighteen-year-old boys with all that ass you hoes toting?" Uzi Mi spat, looking into Ada's cold eyes. He knew one thing: she could have easily been a famous Instagram model, but instead, she'd rather kill niggas for a fee.

She was beautiful, with light freckles across her face. Her body was a weapon; she carried an ass so massive and kinetic that every step she took sent a violent tremor through her hips, making the flesh quake and roll like it was having a seizure. Her dreads hung wildly down her back, a shade of fire-red that matched the scorched-earth hatred she carried in her heart towards men. She despised them all, but she saved a special kind of venom for the ones from her village who dared to touch her.

When she was fifteen, her father had raped her and sold her to a fierce rebel group that made the Mexican cartels look like rookies when it came to executions. They raped her and six other women on the daily, until her beauty caught the eye of a soldier named Bantu. He fell in love with her, and she used her pussy and sweet words to gain his trust. *The pussy is a man's worst enemy.* He eventually killed a dozen of his own brothers just to save her.

After they escaped the concrete jungle, Bantu taught her everything his brothers-in-arms had taught him. He turned her into a killing machine—a bitch not to be fucked with. She was a deadly enemy.

One night, Bantu woke up to her soft lips wrapped around his throbbing dick, sucking it to its full potential. When he finally focused his eyes on his "one and only," she swung a machete across his dick, slicing it clean. She had never heard a man scream the way he did; it was like he was free-falling from the sky or some shit.

Ever since then, she'd been ruthless. Her only mistake was letting Bantu live, but she only did that because he'd freed her from a life of hell. Then again, living without a dick . . . she might as well have killed him.

"We're going to bring his head to you. That's my word," Ada said as she straddled his lap, her heavy weight settling firmly against him. Uzi Mi leaned back, trying to maintain his composure and sip his champagne, but the tension in the room was electric. Lucia leaned in close, her eyes locked on his, as her hand worked with a slow, teasing rhythm, stroking his dick through the silk of his Versace briefs until it was rock-hard and straining against the designer fabric.

***

Outside…

Leroy and Delroy waited patiently outside Ada's crib. They had tailed the two strippers, knowing that sooner or later, Uzi Mi would pop up. They knew those two scandalous bitches were working their magic to lure them to their enemy, but now the truth was right in front of them.

"I told you we should have killed them bitches when we had a chance back at the club," Delroy spat in his deep Haitian accent. He was the original leader of YPB, and even though he was only eighteen, his kills were already legendary; videos of his hits played continuously on websites across the internet.

To his brothers, he was nothing short of a legend. The beef between Delroy and Uzi Mi's uncle was personal—no outsider comes to his city and sets up shop. From drugs to guns, YPB had their bloody hands in everything.

"We can get all of them now," Leroy said. Both boys had been tight since they were little kids back in Little Haiti. At the age of eighteen, Leroy was already responsible for the deaths of over seven people. He was the biggest, toughest eighteen-year-old Delroy had ever known. Leroy was a walking homicide, a natural-born killer who was a fool with his hands, head, knees, and elbows. He didn't just fight; he dismantled men. Leroy was one of the few people Delroy knew, in his soul, he probably couldn't out-scrap in a street fight, but the pride in his Haitian blood meant he'd still die trying. Leroy towered over him by at least four inches and was nearly twice as wide—197 pounds of solid muscle, to be exact. His head was full of wild dreads, and his skin was black as tar. He looked like Ace Hood, but with scars on his face and body from the years of war he'd endured on the streets of Miami. He was a killer in a boy's body.

"Right now?" Delroy asked, looking over at Leroy.

"Hell yeah. Why not?"

Back Inside Ada's Crib…

Ada stood up from the sofa, having ridden Uzi Mi's dick until he was exhausted. She walked over to the wet bar, her ass clapping with a rhythmic, heavy thud like a seal's applause. Lucia took over from where she left off, turning her back to him, her ass doing a fool. Everything about her was amazing. She had it all, a beautiful face and a big-ass booty. And some good-ass pussy.

Ada could feel their eyes on her backside as her soft ass cheeks played *Candy Crush*, smacking against each other with the force of an HBO Pay-Per view fight.

"Give it me, baby," she moaned as she spread her ass cheeks wide open. She was feeding her pussy with his dick. They both were on the verge of climaxing together, when the front door flew from its foundation.

Boc. Boc. Boc.

Three hot slugs from Leroy's Glock hit Lucia in the chest. Uzi Mi didn't have time to grieve; he was just grateful she was positioned as a human shield. He grabbed his Tec-9 beside him and aired some shit out.

Meanwhile, Ada took five bullets to the back as the hitters rushed in blasting. She was dead before she even touched the ground, totally unaware of the danger that had just turned her sanctuary into a slaughterhouse.

Budda-Budda-Budda.

The deafening chatter of the Tec-9 gunfire sent both gangstas scrambling back toward the door. Uzi Mi kept the trigger squeezed, using Lucia's limp, warm corpse as a sandbag. He couldn't get a clean bead on them through the smoke and the chaos.

Uzi Mi jumped up, shoving Lucia's body aside, the adrenaline masking the horror of her blood on his skin. He made to chase his enemies but thought against it. Instead, he went dove for the window, shattering the glass and disappearing into the Miami heat. He knew one thing for certain: shit just got serious. This was a war of extinction. It was him or them, and he wasn't planning on being the one in the dirt.

Chapter 23

Win Or Perish

The black Bentley tore down the strip, tires screaming as Uzi Mi yanked the wheel into a hard left. His chest was heaving, the metallic scent of gunpowder and Lucia's blood clinging to his skin. He still couldn't believe what had just happened.

Was it a set up? Did those bitches lead them straight to the crib?

He'd never know because both of his uncle's killers were dead. He had to get Monsta B, and fast. He pulled out his iPhone and called him.

"What it do?" Monsta B answered on the first ring.

"Them bitch ass niggas tried to kill me." Uzi mi stated vehemently. "They caught me slipping at the spot. It's up now—way up."

On the other side of the phone…

Monsta B stood up from the couch and took a long sigh, shaking his head from side to side. Blood was the only revenge. Somebody was going to die tonight.

He looked at the naked blonde he'd been letting crash at his spot. She was a high-tier Instagram model with a million followers and a set of humongous, gravity-defying titties that seemed to have a life of their own. She was perched on the edge of the leather chair, her thumbs flying across the Xbox controller as she talked shit to someone online. Face-wise, she was a ten—bad as hell—but once she stood up, the illusion faded; her ass was flatter than a Taylor Swift lyric, a complete 180 from the thick-bodied strikers Uzi Mi usually kept around.

"Put some fuckin' clothes on. My boss is on the way over, bitch," Monsta B barked.

"I guess I can, ugh," she said, her titties bouncing all over her chest.

Twenty minutes later…

Uzi Mi and all the heavy hitters from his uncle's inner circle were out of their whips, the engines still idling as they lined up in front of Monsta B's crib. Flanked by Monsta B himself, Uzi Mi stepped into the middle of the concrete circle. He looked like a man who had just walked through hell and was ready to burn the rest of the world down.

"Today is the day we win or perish," Uzi Mi roared, his voice cutting through the humid Miami air. "Strap up, each of you. My uncle out here playing and letting the enemy do what the fuck they wanna do, not me."

Monsta B's white bitch stood in front of about 12 some niggas, recording them on Facebook live. Each man held up gang signs. Mostly G-9.

Uzi Mi stood in the middle talking a whole lot of shit. "Fuck YPB. Fuck Leroy. Fuck Delroy. We out here posted ready for you pussies. Pull up, only one of us could be the last nigga standing. Y'all some bitches. Let's just be real. Delroy, you mad because I fucked yo' babymama. Get out yo' feelings. She chose up with a boss, not a little-ass boy."

The only sound vibrating through the air was the trunk-rattling bass of "Pull Up" blaring in the background, punctuated by the rhythmic, rapid-fire crack of switches hitting like it was the Fourth of July.

Uzi Mi and his uncle's men went ham, laughing and wilding out as they jumped in front of the lens like they were front-row at a YoungBoy concert. They were intoxicated by the adrenaline. "Pull up. Pull up," they continued to shout in the camera, flashing high-capacity sticks and designer heat, mocking the enemies they had just left in the dust.

Delroy was riding with some YPB niggas, the taste of failure bitter in his mouth after catching Uzi Mi slipping and failing to close the deal. His phone vibrated with a call from Biggie, one of his fat hoes. She was messy as hell—the kind of bitch who stayed in everybody's business and made sure she was the first to spread the word.

"What it do, bitch?" he answered, still mad he didn't kill Uzi Mi.

"Where you at, nigga?"

"Riding by the smoke shop in yo' neck of the woods."

"You by Forest Lane? You need to pull up over here. You got to see this. Uzi Mi going live, dissing you and the whole squad."

"Bet money, I'm on the way," Delroy growled. He yanked the wheel, swerving his Tesla into a violent U-turn and heading straight toward Biggie's crib.

Delroy's eyes were red as blood as he stared at the screen in Biggie's hand. The disrespect was loud, and it was viral. He knew he had to end this today—permanently. He called up his niggas and made his way to the door with Leroy and two other hitters. Biggie was close behind. But Delroy's cold voice stopped her in her tracks. "Where the fuck you think you going?" he snapped grimly.

"With you, the fuck," she shot back. Her three homegirls stepped out behind her, all of them rocked out in some sexy-ass gear. Biggie, on the other hand, was built just like her name—*big*. But she moved with the confidence of a thick, fine bitch. With a sassy ass attitude.

"Bitch, you not coming with us. I don't trust yo' fat ass," Delroy spat. "Yeah, I know all about you fuckin' with the other side. You keep it playing both sides of the fence, you gon' die with them."

Chapter 24

Blood Is War

Niggas in Texas might've feared Uzi Mi, but not Delroy. This wasn't Texas; this was Miami, and he was *that* nigga. Behind him, at least seven whips trailed in a tight, aggressive formation, all of them swerving and not giving a fuck about anything but the body count that lay ahead.

Uzi Mi was a boss in Texas, but Delroy was the most feared YN to ever come out of Little Haiti. What Delroy couldn't understand was how Uzi Mi could even be considered a threat when he was out here running from a muthafucka from his own city. *The nigga that's chasing him can thank me later,* Delroy thought, a cold smirk crossing his face. Because as far as he was concerned, Uzi Mi was already a dead muthafucka. No questions asked.

Uzi Mi and his uncle's men were still outside posting videos when a burst of heavy gunfire exploded nearby. All around, G-9 members dove behind parked cars and trees. Some reacted too late, going down bloody and stanking. Uzi Mi dropped to the pavement, dragging the big-titty white bitch down with him. Bullets danced and sparked all around them.

Blocka. Blocka. Blocka.

In the distance, Delroy and his squad hopped out of their whips, chopping shit down like axes. Blood was splashing in every direction. Uzi Mi couldn't believe the body count dropping before his eyes; this shit right here was way worse than any encounter he'd ever had back in Texas.

Monsta B and a couple more gangsta niggas stood their ground, barking back at the opps with their own heat. Uzi Mi's second wind kicked in. He snatched his Tec-9 off the ground and aired that bitch out. *There can only be one.*

"Y'all some bitches!" Delroy screamed, his assault rifle going the fuck off.

Beside Uzi Mi, a handful of his soldiers were at his side poppin' shit off. It was an all-out war in the middle of the hood as lead flew back and forth from both sides.

Blocka. Blocka. Blocka.

Sirens began to wail in the distance, but neither Uzi Mi nor Delroy gave a fuck about anything but killing one another. Somebody had to die. As Delroy and his niggas finally began to retreat, they left a trail of bodies scattered everywhere.

Uzi Mi and Monsta B took off running toward them, still squeezing their triggers, right along with a young, wild nigga reppin' G-9 to the fullest. But despite the lead they threw, Delroy and Leroy managed to get away safe.

Back at Uzi Mi's crib…

Uzi Mi stood there with his chest heaving up and down. The lamp was shattered against the wall, and the nightstand was flipped over. All his jewelry and clothes were laid scattered and thrown on the floor. All done by Jelly hating ass.

He watched her silently as she snatched her clothes out of the walk-in closet. She began throwing them in her designer bags. Uzi Mi reached out and wrapped his arms around her tiny waist. "Baby, you don't got to go."

She turned and looked at him with tears spilling down her face. "I can't. I just can't. Six niggas died because of you. I'm going back to Dallas with you or without." Jelly kissed his lips and made her way out the front door. She passed the hard-looking men, including Monsta B whose designer shirt was still soaked through with a dark, copper-scented blood that didn't belong to him. He opened the door for her and let her by. Her watery eyes met his cold heartless ones. "Please, bring him back to me alive," she choked out, her voice trembling against the silence of the room. Monsta B didn't blink; he just gave a slow, ominous nod. With that, she was gone, throwing ass like Tom Brady in the fourth quarter as she scrambled to her whip and disappeared.

Uzi Mi refused to go back to Dallas when he still had unfinish business right there in Miami. Delroy and Leroy had to die, even if it meant getting killed in the process. He had to end this before he could go back to Dallas and kill Hideous.

He sat there in the shadows, looking out the window at Jelly's taillights as they faded into the distance. He couldn't help but wonder: would she really be waiting for him when he made it back, or would she be a memory once Hideous knew the bitch that gave his sister up was back on the map. He knew it was only a matter of time before some fisherman found her bloated and floating face-down in the murky currents of Trinity River, a single, cold-blooded bullet lodged in the back of her skull.

Chapter 25

Back in the City

It was dark outside as Butt-Butt leaned against the cool, damp brick wall of her apartment building, her chest heaving with a few ragged breaths. Hideous was inside trying to find a magazine clip for his Uzi. She pulled out her iPhone and made a call. After a few rings, she heard a hood-bitch accent she'd been expecting.

"Morning, baby, why are you calling me this late?"

"Brittany," Butt-Butt said.

It felt strange hearing her government name out after so long. "What is it, Morning?"

"Bunz is dead." The words felt like lead. On the other end of the line, Butt-Butt heard Bunz's T-Jones erupt into a soul-shattering scream. She knew she shouldn't have called, but how could she not tell the lady that raised her that her only daughter was dead because they were trying to rob a stash house.

"What the fuck happened?" Brittany shrieked through the phone.

Butt-Butt couldn't find the words. She disconnected the call, the silence of the night rushing back in. That awful phone call was two in a half weeks ago. She remembered it well. It was the same day that Bunz was taken from her.

It was now Friday night, 12:09 a.m. Hideous and Butt-Butt were parked in front of the *Pink House*, the interior of the car thick with the fog potent kush. They sat there in the smoke, watching the spot like hawks, waiting for Flip to arrive.

Hideous was eyeballing one car in particular that had just pulled up near the valet line. It had been two fucking weeks of hunting, and he was desperate to find Flip. At first, Flip was lying low, but eventually, he turned up and came out of hiding. The *Pink House* was where Sabrina had spotted him clubbing.

She'd landed a gig weeks ago at the newest, hottest strip club in the city. She saw him one night when he was throwing money around like he was a millionaire. When he caught sight of her, he looked like he'd seen a damn ghost. Word on the street was she'd been running her mouth to the wrong people about an ACC. When Flip pushed up on her, she fed him a bullshit story about a scarred-up killer. Flip wanted to know everything, but Sabrina gave him nothing but lies.

She told him Hideous had been coming into the club asking about the whereabouts of Uzi Mi's top dawgs. Flip had texted her earlier that day saying he was gonna pop up tonight—and there Hideous sat, staring at another nigga who'd played a part in his sister's untimely death.

At 12:45, Flip walked into the crowded club where strippers slid up and down poles butt-ass naked, their oiled bodies glistening under the dim lights. Two bad mixed-breed twins were on stage; one's ass was jumping a mile a minute, while the other—rocking a blonde mohawk—was squatted low with her legs spread wide, pussy fatter than a muthafucka. She rubbed on it like she was petting a prized dog.

Flip was stuck, mesmerized by the duo known in the industry as Salt and Pepper. He grinned, pulling out a thick wad of cash and raining it down on them. When he ran out of ones, he started launching twenties.

Sabrina emerged from the locker room, surprised to see him rolling dolo. What she didn't know was that Flip wanted some alone time; he knew he couldn't be a snake in front of his niggas. They'd look down on him for messing with her, especially since she was rumored to have gotten Black killed and caused one of Uzi Mi's main stash houses to get sprayed.

She strutted past a bunch of thirsty, broke-ass niggas, her big titties swaying as she moved in nothing but a white G-string that made her ass look extra chunky. She flashed a smile at her two girls as she approached the stage. Flip was still showering the twins with dead presidents.

When he looked up, Sabrina was standing right there. She was showing off her two slugs filled with VVS diamonds. He leaned over and whispered in her ear, "I know what you did, bitch, and my people want you dead. But I can save you."

Sabrina played it off cool. "I don't know what you're talking about."

"Bullshit. You know you got Black killed running yo' mouth to Macy and Indii."

Sabrina was scared as hell, but she had to keep it together. "Like I said, I don't know what you're talking about."

He responded by cupping her fat ass and squeezing her soft cheeks. "If word gets back to my boss that you had something to do with getting Black killed, he's gonna greenlight that hit. But I can make it all disappear." He pulled the crotch of her G-string aside and rubbed her clit. She moaned, and his dick went rock-hard.

The next day, Flip got a call from Uzi Mi telling him Jelly was flying into the city. Uzi wanted her to crash at Flip's crib for a while—just until he murked Delroy and Leroy. Flip was lying across the bed with his hands behind his head, staring down at the goddess before him. Being a nigga who was born with nothing but a dying wish to be a boss, Flip felt his day was coming sooner than he expected. He looked into the eyes of the bitch who promised to give him all that. And in return, she was going to give him Hideous.

Sabrina's head was on a repeat in his lap. She was working her lips and tongue on a dick that had him wanting to moan like a lil' bitch. She was a bona fide Head Hunter, and she proved it as she took him deeper into her mouth, her throat constricting around him until she was buried to the hilt.

Uck-Uck-Uck. The sound was wet and heavy, the unmistakable noise of her fighting to keep from gagging while she slurped and bobbed her head up and down. Flip watched her, his fingers tangled in her hair, feeling every bit of that suction.

He cut his eyes at the other two sleeping beauties on either side of him. They were both naked, just like they'd been back on stage when he first walked into the club. The two twins were simply three words: *bad as fuck.*

He didn't want to leave to go pick up Uzi Mi's bitch, but Uzi was the nigga with the bag. He took one more look at Salt and Pepper and shook his head. They were both exotic as fuck. One rocked a black mohawk and the other a blonde one. They were mixed—their T-Jones was from Costa Rica, and their father was black and dead.

Flip gritted his teeth and closed his eyes. When he opened them again, Sabrina was straddling his lap, about to slide onto his throbbing dick. But Flip stopped her.

"Get the fuck off me!" he spat, caught up in his feelings. He felt like he was being played like a bitch by Uzi Mi. *Who the fuck this nigga think I am? Who I look like—Driving Miss Daisy?* Flip was heated.

"Damn, what's yo' problem?" Sabrina asked.

"I got to go get my boss's bitch."

Sabrina's eyes lit the fuck up. As soon as he left, she made a quick call to Hideous. Jelly was back in the city.

Chapter 26

The Truth about a Killer

Hideous was rolling around with Butt-Butt when his cellular rang, Sabrina's face popping up huge on the screen. He swiped green to open the FaceTime, and Sabrina's image filled the frame. She was clearly naked—all he could see was a wide, mischievous smile and big titties bouncing every which way.

"What it do?" Hideous asked.

"Get over here quick. I got some news you gon' be thrilled about, but I can't talk about it over the phone. I'm 'bout to send you the addy."

Hideous let out a long sigh and turned to Butt-Butt. "Let's go see what this bitch got to say. Just stay ready for anything. My trust is getting real limited."

Butt-Butt's heart had turned pitch-black; she didn't give a fuck about nothing but the next kill. Catching Uzi Mi and erasing his whole team was the only thing on her mind. She gripped her signature weapon—the pistol-grip shotgun Hideous had customized for her—which was tucked right between her thick legs.

Sixteen minutes later…

Hideous and Butt-Butt stepped through the front door of Flip's condo, both with their pieces drawn. As soon as Hideous scanned the room, he spotted two big-booty, small-waist twins that nearly took his breath away. It wasn't just their beauty—it was the fact that they looked exactly like his sister, Rachel. He stood there, literally stuck.

"Damn, bitch, do I got a booga in my nose?" Pepper asked, trying to be funny because of the way he was staring.

"Leave my baby alone," Sabrina said, throwing her arms around Hideous's neck. All three bitches were butt-naked, rotating a blunt among themselves. Hideous tried not to stare, but damn.

"You don't got to be mean to him," Sabrina added. "This is the nigga I been telling y'all about."

"Oh, the one that's trying to kill Uzi Mi?" the other twin with the blonde mohawk asked.

Hideous and Butt-Butt exchanged glances for a fraction of a second. He made a mental note right then to kill Sabrina. A bitch that ran her mouth like that was a liability. As soon as he got to Uzi Mi, she was a wrap.

Hideous pushed her aside, his Uzi braced against his hip as he paced across the enormous living room. He stopped dead in his tracks when one of the twins said, "Bitch, he look just like our pops."

"Rest in peace, Daddy," the other twin said, crossing her arms over her chest like she was Catholic. She was being straight sarcastic.

"Bitch, you mean Jephthah."

Hideous walked over and stopped right in front of them. "What the fuck did y'all just say?"

Salt and Pepper stood up, mugs attached to their faces. "I said you look just like our pops."

"Did you say his name was Jephthah?"

"Yeah, that's his fucking name. You're acting weird," Salt shot back aggressively.

It all hit him like a flash flood. He'd heard his T-Jones crying to Ms. Parker plenty of times about how Jephthah had a secret family. He just never knew *they* were the secret.

"How old y'all is?"

"Twenty-four. Damn, why?" Pepper asked, staring at her twin like, *What this nigga on, asking all these questions?*

Hideous relaxed his posture and lowered his weapon. He looked them in the eyes and saw Rachel staring back at him. He couldn't believe he was standing in front of his own half-sisters. The world was definitely small.

After he broke down who he was and who his T-Jones was, the room went dead silent until Salt spoke up. "So, Jochebed is your mama dukes?"

He nodded, his expression grim. His hands were actually trembling. He'd always wanted to know the truth about the man who fathered him. "Tell me something about him."

"That's easy—he was a killer. Point-blank. Niggas feared him," Pepper barked, still processing the fact that the rumors of her father's other family were true. They talked for another ten minutes before Salt dropped the real bomb.

"To be honest, we don't fuck with your T-Jones. The streets said she had something to do with our pops getting killed. Said she set him up and fed him to a crazy Chinese muthafucka named Suwoo Chan."

"Fuck Suwoo Chan! When we catch up with that muthafucka, his ass is dead!" Pepper spat, her eyes flashing with the same coldness Hideous possessed.

"What beef did he have with Suwoo Chan?" Hideous asked.

"Jephthah robbed a laundromat in East Dallas that Suwoo Chan owned. It was a front for an illegal gambling spot, moving big money and drugs."

"Yeah, our daddy left about six niggas twisted and took a bunch of munyun," Pepper added, throwing her two cents in.

"And you say my T-Jones had something to do with his death? How?"

"Well, our mama dukes said Suwoo Chan put a hundred-thousand-dollar bag on our daddy's head, and your T-Jones lured him to a strip club and handed him over to the enemy."

"But I don't understand why she would do that."

"Like I said, our daddy was a heartless muthafucka. He was abusive as hell to our mama dukes, and they were actually married. I can only imagine what he put yours through."

Sabrina and Butt-Butt sat in silence, listening as the sisters painted a picture of the monster Jephthah Cash really was. He was a menace, a John Gotti in his era. The only thing he loved more than money was pussy, and that was his downfall.

Hideous absorbed it all. He wanted to know why his mother would double-cross a man like that, but more than anything, he wanted that power. He wanted to be feared just like Jephthah Cash.

After a few hours of getting to know Salt and Pepper, Hideous learned they were high-end exotic strippers from Fort Worth. He eventually drifted off, his head in Butt-Butt's lap, until a shuffling sound woke him up. Sabrina was standing by the sofa.

"Y'all got to go," she whispered. "Flip is on his way back with Jelly. I promise to hit you when the coast is clear."

Wiping the slob from his mouth, Hideous sat up and snatched his Uzi off the coffee table. He stood up with his mind racing. Salt and Pepper wanted him to break the code; they wanted him to bite the hand that fed him and help them kill Suwoo Chan. He wondered if that was even possible.

Chapter 27

Addicted To Money

Fat Mama couldn't lie; she was addicted to the money. Ever since she got away with that kidnapping with Lil' T, she'd been itching for another lick. So, why not snatch the bitch at her job who ran her mouth all the damn time about her baby daddy?

Everybody knew Fila's BD was getting serious paper. The bitch walked around with her glued-on ass like she was the shit just because her nigga was hood rich. What Fat Mama didn't get was why the bitch still wanted to pop her pussy in the club every night. She was always in some different nigga's face, spilling her man's business all over the streets. At least with Fat Mama, she was in the club for a reason: to find the muthafucka that killed her own BD. Even though she had Hideous's number, he hadn't texted her in days.

Now, she waited in the back of a windowless van with three of her brothers in front of the Pink House. "There the bitch go," Fat Mama said, pointing at three fake-booty strippers walking out with a fat nigga toting their two giant trash bags.

"Which bitch?" Cain asked, snatching the choppa off the floor.

"The baddest one," Fat Mama shot back.

"They all bad," Mark pointed out.

"The bitch in the middle, damn . . . and who the fuck said you was getting out? Sit yo' ass down!" Fat Mama spat.

Five minutes later…

Fila tried to scream, but her voice came out as a hoarse rasp. Cain turned to face her with the choppa. Although she couldn't see his face behind the ski mask, his eyes were cold and soulless.

"Get that bitch!" Cain barked at his brother, Paul.

Fila felt an arm wrenching her back as Paul snatched her into a headlock, his Glock 19 aimed at the two remaining hoes. The fat black bouncer had both hands high in the air, the two enormous trash bags sitting like ducks near his feet. Cain cut a look at his brother and crept behind the bouncer.

The eyes of Fila and the other two strippers widened with terror. The bouncer felt the shift in the air behind him, but before he could move, Cain swung the choppa like a Louisville Slugger. The man dropped face-first. Cain showed zero mercy, swinging the heavy stock of the rifle relentlessly into the back of the man's skull, crushing bone and brain matter. Cain snatched up one of the bags of money and slung it over his shoulder.

"Bring that bitch and let's go," Cain spat, the AK now leveled at the two fake-booty strippers to keep them frozen.

"Nooooo," was the only sound echoing through the lot as Fila was tossed into the back of the van.

"Why didn't you kill them hoes?" Mark asked as they piled in.

"We need them to spread the word," Cain shot back.

Fat Mama glanced back at Fila, but the girl didn't have a clue who she was with the mask concealing her face. Fat Mama slammed the van into gear and disappeared into the dark city streets.

Across town, a freak bitch named Lala handed 300 a Gucci bag stuffed with $108,000.

"Thanks, bae," he said, his eyes drifting down to the fat pussy-print she had on full display like a new whip on a showroom floor. Her ass was juicy in those white leggings—Lastarya-level juicy.

"You good? Where my bitch, Fila, at?" Lala asked, scouting the enormous luxury apartment. She didn't give a fuck about the girl; she was just being messy.

"My bitch should've been here by now," 300 grumbled, staring at his iPhone. He was surprised to see a video message from an unknown number. "Who the fuck is this?"

He swiped and tapped the clip. It opened to a shot of his baby mama. She had been stripped naked and lashed to a chair, her wrists and ankles bound to the wooden frame with nylon rope looped around her body like a spiderweb.

She looked like a wreck—sobbing, drool leaking from her lips, thick saliva streaking down her bare chest. A small, jagged cut had been opened across the bridge of her nose. She looked into the camera with heartbroken desperation.

"Please, 300, do what they say," Fila mumbled. "They'll kill me if you don't. Don't call the police. They'll be in touch with instructions soon, bae."

Just before the screen went dark, a nigga stepped forward. What happened next almost knocked 300 out of his seat. He watched as the masked gunman whipped out his dick and shoved it down Fila's throat.

"Oh my gawd," Lala gasped, peering over his shoulder.

He played the clip back again and again, his vision tunneling as he tried to figure out who could be this brazen. Who was he beefing with? *Shid, the whole city knows I'm getting money. Could be anybody.* 300 turned to Lala, shaking his head in disbelief at the thought of what Fila was enduring off-camera. In a fit of rage, he slammed his fist through the drywall, his knuckles punching a clean hole through the frame.

"So . . . we sit and wait?" Lala whispered.

"Hell no. I'm about to go find my bitch."

Back at the bando…

Cain pulled his pants back up after nutting all over Fila's face. He knew her baby daddy had seen the video by now. Just as he expected, he heard his sister yelling from the other room. "Let's call the nigga now."

Cain walked out of the room where they were holding Fila and made his way toward the living room of the abandoned house. He rocked a white beater, his muscles rippling through the thin material. He was heavily tattooed and looked every bit the killer he was. He set his gun down and picked up his machete—his favorite weapon next to an AK.

"Boy, what the fuck took you so long? Call him," Fat Mama barked as the phone started ringing.

300 answered on the first vibration. "Yo, this 300. I'm listening."

Fat Mama handed the phone to Cain.

"Ten o'clock tonight. Buckner and Norvell. There's a rim shop that sits on the corner. Be alone. And have two-hundred thousand with ya."

300 looked down at his diamond-encrusted Rolex. *That might be a problem. Not enough time. I got to collect from different spots.* "That might be a problem," 300 said out loud. "Not enough time. I got to collect from different spots."

"Not my muthafuckin' problem, playboy."

"Oh yeah?" 300 said, the image of the mother of his child being disrespected flashing through his mind. He gripped the phone tight enough to crack the screen.

"Do we have an understanding?" Cain asked.

"I'll be there," 300 agreed. "Can I hear her voice?"

Cain looked over at his sister and smiled, knowing it was about to be another big payday.

Chapter 28

Thunder And Lighting

Three days at Flip's crib, and Jelly had gotten comfortable real quick—walking around half-naked in short tight jeans, boyshorts, and sometimes nothing at all. Flip couldn't get the bitch out of his mental. One night, he was playing *Madden 26* when Sabrina came in and sat next to him. She knew she had to move fast; Hideous was starting to get real impatient. She knew she needed to make her move.

Sabrina had her Chrissy Teigen-shaped titties on full display. When Jelly stepped into the room, Flip bumped Sabrina's arm, trying to get her attention. She already knew what he wanted. He wanted his boss's bitch.

"Girl, do you ever wear a bra?" Jelly asked as she strutted toward the stairway with Flip's eyes fixated on her fat chocolate ass.

Flip looked over at Sabrina and nodded as if to say, *Bitch, make yo' move.* He looked back at Jelly; he could see her juicy ass cheeks peeking out from under her small T-shirt. He could only imagine her not wearing any panties.

"Not when you're around, I'm not," Sabrina shot back, following behind as Jelly walked up the stairs.

Jelly looked over her shoulder at the top of the stairway. "What I tell you last time you tried to flirt with me? I'm not a fuckin' dyke."

She kept walking, her ass jigglin' harder than a bitch. She knew Sabrina's eyes were glued to her, so she gave her something to look at. She slowly lifted her T-shirt over her hips, revealing exactly what Sabrina was desperately trying to see. Her shaved pussy and her fat ass were something different. "Here . . . you see it?"

Sabrina waved her off but continued to follow her until they made it to the bedroom. Jelly's shirt was still pulled up, giving her a show. Her ass jiggled so much it was like watching a booty-shaking video on TikTok.

"Damn, bitch, is you gon' follow me all the way inside the room?" Jelly stopped and faced her.

"I'm just trying to see what's up between them legs." Sabrina stuck her tongue out like Megan Thee Stallion.

"Not ever going to happen. If I let you taste my pussy, you're going to leave yo' nigga."

"I can't help it—you sexy as hell to me." Sabrina lifted the front of Jelly's shirt, getting a perfect view of her bald pussy.

"Let me get dressed. Flip is still taking me to the mall, right?"

"Yeah . . . if you let me taste it," Sabrina said with a smile.

"Bitch, don't play with me," was the last thing Jelly said before stepping into her room and closing the door.

Close to an hour later…

Jelly sat with her legs crossed, her short designer dress riding up her thick thighs. She didn't look at Sabrina or Flip as she tugged gently at the fabric. She was clearly trying to be patient while Flip finished his game. He was being straight petty, making her wait just because she took half an hour to get ready—even though she'd only put on a short-ass dress. But a bitch had to wash her ass and everything.

Sabrina came over and took a seat opposite her, eyeing her from head to toe. She watched Jelly cross and recross her legs slowly. Jelly noticed Sabrina's eyes wandering, so she slid her hand between her thighs to hide her pussy from view.

"Girl, what are you doing?" Jelly asked as Sabrina moved in and sat right next to her.

"Bitch, you know you want it," Sabrina said, licking her neck and ear. She was a master at getting what she wanted, and right now, she wanted Jelly to submit right in front of Flip.

Before she knew it, Jelly was draped across Sabrina's lap with her dress hiked up to her hips. Jelly looked back at Flip as he paused the game and made his way over. Sabrina reached down and grabbed Jelly's soft ass cheeks in each hand.

Meanwhile…

Hideous had to end whatever beef he had with Detective Mark D. Anthony. He watched as Butt-Butt slipped a stylish blonde wig over her head.

"Ass fat, right?" she said, standing in front of the mirror and admiring her sexy naked reflection.

"Just get the job done," Hideous said grimly. His iPhone rang for the umpteenth time. *Damn, Sabrina blowing a nigga up,* he thought as he looked at her pretty face appearing on the huge screen. He knew she was calling about the diamonds, but since his twin sister wanted him to go against the code and give up Suwoo Chan, he doubted he'd ever sell them. Until then, Sabrina needed to stay focused on Jelly.

Butt-Butt was dressed to impress in an all-black, ultra-short Prada dress that made her 52-inch ass stick out like the back of an RV. Her black leather Gucci heels matched her black Ka'oir lipstick. Her nails and toes were midnight black to match. She was ready to kill the detective.

Hideous followed her from the bedroom to the living room. He lifted her dress just to watch her ass jump around as she walked ahead of him. She felt the breeze on her exposed flesh as she proceeded toward the front door. When she reached the threshold, she finally pulled the fabric down.

"I'll be waiting in the car," she tossed over her shoulder.

As soon as she walked away from the house, Hideous dialed a familiar number with a smirk on his face. He listened as a woman's voice invaded his ear. “Yes, he’s still out there in front of your old house.”

“Damn, wassup? You good?”

“Yeah, it’s just you blowing my phone up.”

“Sarah, chill. I’ll be over there when this shit is over with. I’m gon’ chill by your spot, if that’s cool with you.”

“Why wouldn’t it be?”

“Have you heard from your brother?”

“Why? So you can kill him?”

“Naw, I told you we got back cool,” he lied smoothly.

“Bullshit . . . since my brother been smoking that shit, he don’t got time for nobody.”

“We good now. I hope the nigga the best.” Hideous grabbed his Uzi and walked out the door. He kept the phone to his ear as he hopped into Butt-Butt’s black Range Rover—the one she’d won for taking first place at Poleathon years back.

“Whateva. Just come see me while I’m in town. I’m leaving soon, going back to college.”

“I got ya.” Hideous disconnected and looked over at Butt-Butt.

“Nigga, you don’t got to get off the phone,” she snapped. “We in this to kill a sworn enemy, nothing more.”

“Just drive.”

27 minutes later…

Detective Mark D. Anthony was posted up in front of Hideous’s T-Jones’s old house, the same spot where he’d caught him before. He was praying the son of a bitch would show up again. He knew he probably wouldn’t, but what the fuck else did he have to do—work? Killing the bastard who murdered his father was the only "work" he was interested in putting in. He’d sit there until his hair grew back if he had to, but he wouldn't have to wait that long. Hideous had a surprise for him.

Mark watched as a big-booty black bitch in a tight black dress hopped out of a black Range Rover. She made her way up to the front door, tugging her dress down as she walked. She knocked, but got nothing. No answer.

At the exact moment she headed back to the car, Mark pulled his unmarked unit in front of the house. She just stared as he slid down the window.

"Ma'am, you looking for somebody in particular that stayed here? This house is on the market. I'm the realtor, and the buyer is on her way—and she's white, no offense." He lied, trying to bait her to see who she really was.

"I don't need shit! Get the fuck up out my business," she shot back before hopping into her whip.

She drove a few blocks over, stopping in front of Mark's parents' crib, and got out. She leaned into the window and told Hideous, "He 'bout to pull up now. Wait until I get to the door, then we both light his ass up like a Christmas tree." With her designer bag in hand, she had her Glock 19 tucked inside, ready to spray Mark down like a graffiti artist.

Mark followed, trying to control himself as he felt his blood start to boil. *Who the fuck is this bitch? And why the fuck is she heading toward my parents' home?*

"Excuse me, ma'am, this is private property. This crib belongs to me and my family, and you're trespassing." Mark was only an inch away when Butt-Butt spun around, a Glock gripped in her hand.

"What, bitch? What was you saying?"

Mark didn't know what the fuck was happening until he heard the voice of the man he wanted to kill rise up behind him. "Fuck you and yo' daddy!"

Hideous's Uzi sounded like thunder and lightning.

Budda-Budda-Budda!

The bullets ripped through Mark's shoulder, shredding the flesh and peeling it away from the bone. The next burst tore through his neck. He stumbled back, collapsing on the pavement—hitting the exact same spot where his old man had died nine years ago. He tried to move, trying to fight off the inevitable crawl of death. He looked up and saw Hideous in an all-black hoodie, standing over him next to the big-booty bitch dressed like a hooker.

"Fuck . . . you . . ." Mark mumbled tearfully, the copper taste of blood filling his mouth.

Hideous aimed the Uzi at his face, and without a second of hesitation, he squeezed the trigger. The weapon jumped in his hand.

Budda-Budda-Budda.

Chapter 29

Lester Street

Fat Mama popped in her AirPods Pro and locked in on her favorite rapper, TTM Toolie. She stood in the doorway, watching as her brother jerked Fila out of bed butt-ass naked.

"What the fuck are you doing?" Fila shrieked as she was hauled out of the house, slung over his shoulder like a sack of grain.

Fat Mama followed Cain outside, the heavy bass of "12.5/650" thumping in her ears. She watched as he threw Fila into the back. Once the door slammed shut, they both ripped their ski masks off. James and Mark stepped out of the house, choppas in hand. Mark handed his piece to Cain.

"Let's go get this money!" Cain barked, the metallic clack echoing through the night as he cocked the AK back.

10:02 P.M.

Fat Mama watched as a black 1975 Lincoln Continental pulled up in front of the rim shop. She was standing in front of her two brothers, Cain and James. Fila was on her knees next to her, a black pillowcase over her head. Her juicy titties were on full display like art at an exhibit.

300 couldn't believe what he was witnessing. These crazy muthafuckas were on some cartel-type shit. They didn't give a fuck that they were on a main street with cars slowing down to be nosy. He hopped out of the Lincoln with a Goyard bag in his hand.

"Is it all there?" Fat Mama asked.

"Yeah." 300 was surprised to hear a bitch's voice behind the ski mask, but he wasn't surprised she was thick as hell in those tight black leggings. She nodded at Cain, stepped up, and yanked the bag from 300's hand. She opened it and saw nothing but hunchoes.

Three days after getting at 300, Fat Mama was back in the strip club shaking ass and big ol' titties. Her naked body was glistening in baby oil, and she had every eye in the club on her—including Big T's runner, Vezzo. He was there the night she left with Lil' T. She was supposed to be dead, but there she was, acting a fool on a pole.

She was a pro, too. Her taut legs were wrapped around the brass, holding on with one hand. She released her grip and swung upside down, one hooked knee keeping her in place as she did trick after trick. When she got back on all tens, she noticed the hate on the other strippers' faces, but she only cared about the smiles on the hustlers. They were the ones paying the bills. Among the crowd throwing money, one face stood out: Vezzo. He was a ruthless nigga who ran with Big T, and he looked like he was about to jump right into his phone to report back. At the same time, she looked over and saw Hideous.

The *Pink House* was more hood than upscale. The lights were dimmed, and the stages featured bitches shaking more ass than keys on a janitor's belt. Fat Mama wobbled that big caramel ass of hers even harder once she saw the man of the hour.

Butt-Butt threw her arm around Hideous and took a hit from the exotic blunt they'd been sharing. She gazed at Fat Mama on stage and frowned. "I swear I'll shut this bitch down if she's the competition. The bitch don't even got no rhythm," she said, exhaling a cloud of smoke. Butt-Butt walked over to the stage just as Fat Mama was being replaced by another jumbo-booty stripper who was making that thang clap like it was her birthday. She was Ari Fletcher-bad, and even Butt-Butt had to give the girl her roses.

Fat Mama showed Hideous to VIP. She knew she had to move fast because Vezzo's eyes were tracking her every move. She pushed Hideous into the love seat and straddled his lap, grinding her pussy against him. She wrapped her arms around his neck, loving the way his bustdown Cuban rubbed against her skin. She pushed her tits in his face as he cupped her ass, savoring the softness. He almost lost his mind when she did the splits in his lap and started bouncing like a rabbit.

The crowd faded. Even Vezzo disappeared from her mind. Hideous became her only audience. She forced a smile, but he looked at her the way a lion sizes up a gazelle. His jaw clenched whenever her ass clapped together. He pulled out a tight roll of bills and began pouring dead presidents on her.

Unbeknownst to her, he knew for sure now that she was the bitch who had fought his sister years ago. *Just like Detective Mark D. Anthony, she's gonna be another body I have to bury with the rest of my past.*

***

Outside the club…

Judah and his entourage walked down the block toward the club. When they got to the front, they saw a line curving around the side of the building, but they didn't give a fuck. They cut the whole line, wishing a nigga would say something.

Judah was *that nigga* now. With his cut of the kidnapping money, he'd re-upped his supply from the plug. He was moving twice what he'd handled before—forty to sixty kilos at a time. Before the lick, he was getting a minimum of three or maybe six; now, he was in the big leagues.

He had his brothers and seven of his main buyers out to celebrate. A long hallway led them into the main room, which smelled of stale pussy and washed-up weed. Cain was bumping and shoving whoever was in his path as they headed straight for the dance floor, ready for whatever.

The *Pink House* was packed with strippers and niggas everywhere. On stage, Judah spotted an Asian girl who popped ass like a sista. She was working the hell out of the pole, gripping the brass and spinning until her little skirt flew up. She let her hands slide over her body, arching back and drawing every gaze to her fat ass. She made a show of bouncing nonstop while her eyes scanned the perimeter. That's when she saw Judah looking like a million bucks, rocked out in dreads and designer gear, his jewelry gleaming like the real deal.

When he made his way to the stage with a stack of money in hand, she crawled toward him like he was her master.

Cain looked around and spotted his sister. He bumped James's arm and nodded toward Fat Mama, who was giving an X-rated dance to a nigga in a black hoodie that concealed his features. On the other stage, when Rac Yun made it to the edge, she opened her legs to give Judah and his team a full view of a juicy, bald pussy. As she put that ass in Judah's face, he felt a hand tap his shoulder. He turned around and mugged the intruder.

"What it do?" he asked aggressively.

"Look over there at our sister in VIP," Cain said.

"That's her job, silly-ass nigga. Don't come at me with all that bullshit. I'm trying to celebrate."

Judah was letting the money get to his head. He was becoming more out of control, just like his younger brothers, and Cain was starting to take notice. Judah was starting to treat them like his workers, even though they were the ones getting their hands dirty for real while he sat back and collected. He felt unstoppable. He had six trap houses booming, plus the money, jewelry, hoes, and cars.

Cain spun around and saw his sister getting it in. From where he stood, it looked like she was straight-up fucking the nigga in the hoodie. He tapped James and said, "Let's get at this clown and rob him. Fuck what Judah is on."

James nodded, his eyes cold. As the brothers began weaving through the packed crowd toward the VIP section, Hideous was already taking things to a different level. He wasn't just watching anymore; he was taking ownership. He pulled Fat Mama closer, his hands migrating from her waist to the sensitive skin of her inner thighs, claiming territory while the club's bass vibrated through their bones.

"Open," Hideous commanded, his voice a low, jagged growl against her ear.

She obeyed, spreading her knees and exposing everything. He pressed his palm between her legs, cupping her pussy. He found her clit and started rubbing in brutal, demanding circles. Fat Mama lost her breath, rocking her hips against his hand as the friction sent sparks through her core. He pushed one finger inside, then two, then three, stretching her wide until she whimpered.

He abruptly withdrew his fingers and shoved them in her mouth. "Suck 'em clean."

She did as she was told, her lips wrapping tight around his fingers. He pulled them out with a wet pop, then shoved her face down to his crotch. "Go on. Handle that"

She sucked him in, slow and deep. Hideous kept a hand on the back of her head, steering her until she gagged. She tried not to choke, but his dick was huge, hitting the back of her throat with every pulse. She set a rhythm—out, then in, then deeper—even as tears began stinging her eyes. He began to fuck her face with raw violence. Her nose was mashed against his dick hairs as he gripped her head, twisting her hair into a leash to hold her in place. Fucking her face brutally, he was punishing her and pleasing her all at once. And that's how Cain and James caught her. When Hideous looked up, he saw two niggas heading his way with murder in their eyes. He tapped Fat Mama, and she looked up, her makeup smeared and her eyes wide, as she spotted her brothers coming.

"Fuck . . . my brothers," She gasped, scrambling to her feet.

"Yo' brothers." Hideous and Butt-Butt hopped up instantly, their predatory instincts screaming. Hideous remembered the carnage he did in DG's the night he caught his sister dry-humping some nigga; he knew this specific brand of "brotherly" anger. He'd just had his dick in their sister's mouth. And by the looks on their faces, he could tell they weren't coming over to greet him.

Fat Mama's eyes shot past her brothers and locked onto a new nightmare: Big T and his son were storming in the club with a bunch of niggas. "Fuck. Cain, shoot," she screamed, causing her brothers to pull out their weapons like they were in Mexico or some shit.

Cain looked back and let his Glock go the fuck off. He hit a nigga advancing on him. James joined in catching Big T completely off guard. His men weren't even packing no heat. They thought Fat Mama was helpless. He dragged his son to the floor, crawling toward some cover. He looked in horror as Vezzo's body jerked like a marionette, stumbling back before falling dead on the floor.

Fat Mama turned to aim one of her brother's guns at Hideous, but he was already gone. "Fuck," she shrieked.

She redirected her rage, turning the gun on a nigga across the floor and busting shots through his flesh, wishing with every trigger pull that it was Hideous instead. She knew right then her days working at *Pink House* were over. She vowed the next time she saw Hideous, he was dead. Point-blank. A bullet to his head.

Chapter 30

Don't Get Caught By The Camera

Fat Mama learned that four people had died—including a well-known rapper whose career was just starting to take off. None of them, however, was Big T. She took a seat in an armchair, commanding her brothers' undivided attention as she prepared her words carefully.

"Four muthafuckas died and none of them was Big T. This should be a lesson: let's stay out the spotlight and stop partying for a while. Fuck these hoes. Let's just continue to get this money," she said, her gaze fixed mostly on Judah.

She turned her full attention to him. She saw the look of a boss nigga—one determined to eat at all costs. Since he was a youngin', she knew he was their way out; he was always hungry for the paper. When she first started stripping, she began feeding him info on niggas with money who liked to stunt in the club for bitches they didn't even know.

"Judah, promise me something," she said, a flash of hurt in her eyes.

"What, Mama?"

She paused. All her little brothers had the habit of calling her that. It had carried a lot of weight at first, but she'd grown used to it. She had done what most little girls couldn't do: she'd turned boys into men.

"Continue to get money at every cost. Don't matter what you encounter—grind and get yours."

The next morning…

A volley of bullets shook the walls of the bedroom, and the windows exploded in a hailstorm of broken glass. Fat Mama lunged for her son and rolled off the bed. She landed hard on her right shoulder, quickly shifting her weight so she was positioned on top of the boy, shielding him with her own body. Her instincts screamed at her to get to her weapon. She could hear her brothers in the other rooms as they returned fire, the house erupting into a war zone. All she wanted to know was: *What the fuck is happening?*

Before the shooting…

Big T was behind the wheel of one of the black Chevrolet Tahoes, while three others followed close behind. Lil' T was riding shotgun, directing his old man to Fat Mama's crib—the spot he used to go to with Cain when they were younger. He pointed with his Draco toward the house. It was her T-Jones's old place.

"Shoot, nigga. Shoot." Big T barked at him.

Without warning, Lil' T stuck the Draco out the window and shredded the house.

Niggas hopped out toting either a Draco or an AK. They ran up the driveway like trained hitmen, stopping just a few inches from the porch before they lit the house up like a light switch.

Budda-Budda-Budda.

Budda-Budda-Budda.

Big T's men poured lead through the front windows, rocking the entire structure with a hail of bullets.

Back inside…

Only one name came to mind: Big T.

Getting to her feet, she stayed low and made a beeline for the stairs, toting her son. He'd pissed himself by the time they hit the final landing. She saw the damage—bullet holes shredded the floors and the walls. The first thing she thought about was her brothers. Despite the adrenaline pumping through her blood, her lungs felt like wet noodles.

Her brothers stood around the living room at different angles of the windows, returning fire to the opps surrounding the house. Cain held a pump-action shotgun. The blasts were so loud it felt like the world was about to end.

"Get Lil' Max outta here," Cain barked, continuing to blast the gauge.

Fat Mama's breathing became heavy as she fled into the kitchen. She dove under the counter as the fireworks continued. Chaos poured into the streets as Big T's men retreated to their whips. James and Judah's guns went the fuck off. Cain gritted his teeth and tightened his grip on the shotgun; he raised his aim and stepped out of the house, busting that big muthafucka.

Unfortunately, the two Tahoes sped away, jumping the curb as they made their speedy escape. All three brothers ran out of the house, still shooting. There were two fallen men left behind, bodies twisted on the ground.

Chapter 31

Your Worst Nightmare

"Come in," Jelly said, hearing a soft knock at the door. Sabrina opened the door and peeked inside. Jelly was on all fours with her back arched and her ass in the air, deep in her daily workout routine. She shifted into a push-up position right there on the rug. Sabrina stood in the open doorway licking her lips. She had already told Flip that trying to fuck her was a dead issue; she wasn't feeling the idea of fucking "the work"—to her, Jelly was a package to be delivered, not a snack to be sampled.

Unbeknownst to them both, they were all in grave danger. Salt and Pepper were fucking Flip's lights out at that very moment, ready to kill him at any second.

Sabrina crouched down behind Jelly. She pulled Jelly's tights down, exposing her fat ass, and spread her cheeks apart like she was opening a door. She pressed her tongue against her, flat and wet. She gave it a few licks before Jelly cried out.

"Oh, shit," Jelly moaned, squirming on all fours. She tried to pull away from Sabrina's ruthless tongue, but the girl had her going crazy.

"I got a surprise for you, and no, it's not with Flip. This nigga's dick is twelve inches long and thick."

"What'd I tell you? I'm not cheating on my man."

"Flip sent me this to encourage you to fuck with him." Sabrina pulled out her iPhone and scrolled to the videos he'd sent. One featured two girls; he had one of them leaned over a balcony rail, enjoying the view while he was beating some shit in.

"Turn that shit off. I feel like a fool. I been over here being faithful to this dog-ass nigga." Jelly closed her eyes and took a deep breath.

"Flip sent me some more. Do you wanna see them?"

"You said this nigga you got for me got a twelve-inch dick? I just wanna see it." At that moment, Jelly didn't give a fuck if Flip came in and showed his hand. She was hurting on the inside.

"You got to put this blindfold on, though." Sabrina handed it over.

"Why? That shit's weird."

"I told you, it's a surprise."

"Okay, tell him don't be on no weird shit. All I wanted to do was see it." Jelly took the blindfold and slipped it over her eyes. She climbed onto the bed and laid flat on her stomach, burying her face in the pillow.

Sabrina stepped out and came back in with Hideous. He'd been waiting in the car with his Uzi sitting on his lap, finally ready to get his revenge. He'd left Butt-Butt in the car to be his eyes and ears, and he even had his sisters waiting for his signal.

He grabbed her hips and shoved himself inside—all the way—in one hard thrust. Jelly choked on her breath. He fucked her hard, the sound of skin on skin echoing through the room. He slapped her ass, the sting blooming purple on her chocolate skin. He reached around, found her clit, and rubbed it mercilessly.

"Ouch. Oh shit. Oh shit." Jelly couldn't feel anything but that dick being rammed into her. It felt like she was going to pass out. She had to see who the fuck was putting it down like that. She ripped the blindfold off and looked back.

She almost had a heart attack. It was Rachel's brother. Her pussy started squirting like she was pissing when he leveled the Uzi at her face. She was living her worst nightmare.

Hideous had her pussy stretched like a rubber band. She didn't make another sound. She just remained silent, knowing death was about to claim her soul. She looked back at Sabrina, who just watched. Hideous smacked her ass with the barrel of the Uzi, then pressed the cold steel to the back of her head. With his free hand, he gripped the back of her neck and fucked her with a vengeance.

In the other room…

"God, baby, you feel so good," Salt breathed as she began bouncing up and down on Flip's dick, her ass jiggling with every stroke. He squeezed a cheek in each hand, watching his dick slide in and out of her pussy.

He had just fucked Pepper to sleep—or so he thought. She lay next to the action, waiting for the signal to make their next move. Flip looked lost in a trance as Salt rode the shit out of his dick, her ass bouncing in every direction. He had to admit, she was riding that thing like La La Anthony did Ghost on *Power*.

He felt his nut rising, but too bad he wouldn't be able to enjoy it. The sound of gunfire from the other room caught him by surprise, but the twins didn't flinch. That was the signal they'd been waiting for. Pepper hopped up, gripping a Glock 17 she'd tucked under the pillow. Unlike her sister, she already had two bodies to her name—and she was about to claim a third.

When Hideous looked up, Salt and Pepper were marching Flip into the bloody room. He was butt-naked, his hands trying to cover his business. Fear flashed in his eyes as he looked at Jelly's corpse. He scanned the room, seeing Sabrina, Butt-Butt, and his worst nightmare: Hideous.

Sabrina recorded the whole scene for Uzi Mi using Flip's own phone. Flip shook with terror, turning his head away from the sight of the bullet holes in Jelly's flesh. He looked back at Hideous, who was staring him down with cold eyes.

"Y'all killed the one person I loved more than anybody in this fucking world. Y'all took my one and only. My other half. Y'all killed my sister," Hideous growled. He pressed the Uzi to Flip's forehead as Salt and Pepper forced him to his knees. Sabrina watched intently through the screen of the phone.

"Ple—plea—please. I had nothing to do with her death," Flip cried, but it was too late for apologies. He was shivering uncontrollably, but Hideous didn't give two fucks. He looked down at him in pure disgust. A loud bang echoed through the room; the bullets tore into Flip's face, stripping the meat from the bone and leaving him wearing a mask of blood.

"Holy shit," Sabrina screamed, her voice cracking.

Hideous waited until she calmed down, then nodded at her to send the video to Uzi Mi's phone. Once he saw the "Sent" notification, he gave Butt-Butt the signal. She was standing behind Sabrina with a shotgun in her hand. She pressed the barrel to the back of the girl's head and pulled the trigger. Sabrina's head burst open, her skull shattering into a thousand pieces, sending blood, bone, and brain matter scattering across the room.

"Damn, what the fuck." Salt and Pepper chorused, confused, jumping back from the splatter.

Hideous walked over to where Sabrina lay. "A bitch that talk a lot can't be trusted. If you tell my business once, you'll tell it again."

Chapter 32

Double Murder On Haskell

"Damn, bro, look at this," Mark said, thrusting his iPhone at Cain. "Look at this bitch." Cain took the phone and stared at the picture of a half-naked, exotic-looking girl. She was sitting on a bathroom counter, ass facing the camera. He read the name attached to the profile: @GoddessTwin_Salt.

"She feeling me, bro. We been up all night going back and forth with messages. I even called the bitch and we been chopping it up for hours. I'm telling ya, money give a young nigga power. Ever since I posted that money spread picture, shit been going crazy in my DMs."

Cain looked deep into his brother's eyes. He wanted to tell him she was only in it for the bag, but he knew his brother already knew that. Some niggas were just born simps. He wasn't hating, though; the bitch was super bad. She'd seen the money and saw a come-up in a YN.

Unbeknownst to them, Hideous had put his sister on the youngest brother of the bunch, knowing he'd fall for the bait easiest. Hideous hadn't originally known Fat Mama had brothers, but the shootout at the club had opened his eyes to investigate her story. After scrolling through her social media, he'd learned more than enough.

He knew Judah was the oldest and the one getting the real money—Butt-Butt had informed him on that. She said Judah loved to trick with bad bitches and had plenty of paper, but he was far from stupid. Then there were James and Cain;

they were the pawns, doing whatever Fat Mama or Judah said. That left the youngest: Mark. He was the weakest and most vulnerable.

"Be careful, lil' nigga. That's all I'm saying," Cain warned.

"You don't want to come with me? She got a sister."

"Naw, I'm good. You know we got to wait for Fat Mama to get back. She still out looking for a new spot for us. We can't stay in these Budget Suites forever."

"Well, when the bitch calls telling me to pull up, I'm gone—with you or without you."

Fat Mama walked into the room to find Cain and Mark dressed like they were hitting the club.

"What it do, sis?" Mark said elatedly.

"Hey, baby," she replied, a perplexed look on her face. "Where y'all going?"

"Helping James with the rest of the shit back at the old house," Mark lied. He knew she'd said to keep a low profile, but the bait was too sweet.

"Well, hurry back. I got shit I got to take care of." Fat Mama knew she had to meet Hideous later. She'd been surprised to find his text buried among the 670 unread messages in her phone. He'd told her he wanted to make love to her and asked her to meet him at the Omni Hotel so they could finally be alone. She wasn't about to miss the chance to kill him this time. She vowed on her soul he was a dead man. *I'm gon' ride the shit out his big-ass dick,* she thought, *then I'm gonna kill him.*

An hour later, Fat Mama went her way, and her two brothers went theirs, all of them heading toward an early grave.

She pulled up to the Omni and watched as the valet parked her Lexus. She checked her bag for the third time, making sure her Glock 43—a gift from Judah—was ready. The Omni was an endless dream. Fabulous. The good life.

She gazed around the magnificent lobby, realizing she was finally getting the revenge she craved.

She took the elevator to the 23rd floor. Being that far up, she felt like she'd escaped it all—Big T, the kidnappings, and even the stress of the money. She finally felt free. But not completely. She still had to deal with Hideous. She knocked on the door and waited. After a minute, her blood boiled and her jaw tightened as he opened the door and closed it behind her.

"Wow," she breathed. The Presidential Suite was like a palace. Fresh roses everywhere. Complimentary champagne and macarons. A view of half of Dallas. The floor-to-ceiling windows revealed more than just the city; the whole world called out to her.

She looked into one of the bedrooms; it was twice the size of her living room, the walls decorated with expensive artwork. She took a peek into the bathroom—a marble and ivory-colored tub and a shower big enough for a small family.

"This is amazing," she said to Hideous. He was shirtless in a pair of Gucci briefs. He had a bust down Cuban chain connected to a replica of his sister's face hanging down his neck in complete diamonds. She, on the other hand, rocked some tight leggings with a small halter top, her ass poking out like the back of a school bus. She went over to the table, where Hideous had a blunt rolled up. She picked it up and walked over to him. Her titties and ass were bouncing.

"Take that shit off." He couldn't wait to touch, lick, and fuck her.

"I will when I'm done," she said, trying to look anywhere but at him. As she smoked, she peeled her leggings off, leaving on just the shirt. She wanted to get him out the way quickly. She wanted to blow his head off as soon as he opened the door, but the Uzi in his hand made her reconsider. She walked slowly to the counter, placing her purse on top of it where she could reach it.

"I don't like repeating myself. I said take all that shit off."

"Nigga," she said, her mouth was dry as sandpaper. He licked his lips and leaned forward, elbows on the table, hands folded. Then he stood up, the chair sliding back. He crossed the room in three strides, faster than she thought possible. He grabbed her jaw, finger digging in hard, forcing her head back to stare up at him.

His voice was low, deadly. "Bitch, I'm not to be played with."

"Nigga, you need to calm down. It ain't that serious." He yanked her by the wrist and twisted her arm behind her back, pinning her to the wall with his body. His other hand closed around her throat. He yanked the straps to her halter top down until her tits spilled out. He palmed one of her breasts while aggressively sucking the other one and squeezing hard enough to leave marks. Before she could catch her breath, he grabbed her by the waist and spun her around, slamming her chest-front against the wall. He jammed her arms above her head and held them there, his body pressing into her back. Her bare ass was just sitting in the air, big and swollen, caught in the glow of the penthouse lights.

He pulled his boxers down and freed his dick, already hard and leaking. He shoved inside in one punishing thrust. She screamed, high and sharp, 12 inches stretching her walls. The pain was agony. He fucked her hard, each stroke a punishment. He knew she was gunning for him.

Her nails dug into the drywall. She could feel the hate in every stroke, like he knew who she was this whole time. He wrapped her hair around his fist, yanking her head back. Her pussy was slippery. He had to admit she was taking it like a pro.

"Oh, you taking this dick, huh?" he choked out. He grunted, slapping nothing but ass. He bit her shoulder savagely when he started fucking her harder. His dick was flying in and out of her pussy at lightning speed.

He spread her ass cheeks apart so he could dig deeper. He felt her flexing her pussy around his dick like a small hand squeezing. He shuddered, his hips stuttering, then he bust with a roar, burying himself to the hilt. He stayed there, pinned against her, while she fought the urge to vomit. His poison was swimming inside her.

When he finally pulled out, she slid to the floor, her legs too shaky to hold her weight. He stood over her, chest heaving, his dick still dripping. She scrambled to her feet and found her tights, pulling them hoes on with trembling hands as she caught her reflection in the window. *It's time to kill this nigga.* She moved toward the counter, nearly stumbling as she reached for the Uzi, her ass jiggling with every frantic step.

She leveled the piece at him, not knowing the chamber was empty. "I've been waiting for this day for a long time. You took something valuable from me. I been trying to kill you since I first saw you in the club—I even sucked your dick and gave you some pussy just for this moment right here."

Hideous just smiled at her. She squeezed the trigger, but there was no response—only the hollow *click-click-click* of a dry firing pin.

"Now, Butt-Butt!" Hideous barked.

Butt-Butt stepped out of the closet, a shotgun leveled at the room. She walked over and snatched the empty Uzi from Fat Mama's hand. Hideous shoved Fat Mama to the ground hard, leaving her sprawled in a fucked-up position. He grabbed his phone.

"You should've just let me be. Your baby daddy been dead this fucking long," he growled. He opened a message and shoved the screen in her face. Her eyes went wide. She saw her two brothers, Cain and Mark, tied up but still breathing.

"What the fuck," she screamed, her mind racing to grasp the betrayal. Her blood was boiling, her cheeks flushing with pure rage. She went off. “You’re a fucking bitch. Fuck your dead-ass sister.”

Those were the last words she ever spoke. A loud roar boomed through the suite, the sound bouncing off the solid walls. The crack of the shotgun thudded through the air, the recoil rattling Butt-Butt’s frame.

The blast tore through Fat Mama’s torso. Her chest exploded outward, shredded in all directions. She was dead on contact, her life leaking onto the expensive penthouse floor from her ruined chest.

Two days later…

As soon as Judah got the text, he hopped into his whip with James right behind him. Now, he was feeling just like the victims they’d kidnapped: alone and vulnerable. He was certain this was the handiwork of Big T.

He drove at breakneck speeds to the address sent to his phone. It hadn't been hard for Hideous to find him; Judah was mutual friends with Butt-Butt on Instagram and had even been sitting in her DMs on "unread" for weeks.

As soon as they reached the location, Judah's heart dropped into his stomach. His baby brother, Mark, was hanging upside down by his feet, butt-ass naked. His hands were tied behind his back, a deep gash carved through his neck, and a single bullet hole sat between his eyes. His dick had been hacked off and was missing.

Judah and James stepped further into the house. In the middle of the room sat Cain’s dismantled corpse. The bitter, metallic scent of death hit Judah’s nose instantly. They’d cut both of his hands off and sliced his stomach open, his insides leaking out of the wound. It was a good thing Judah had on dark shades; they hid the tears spilling down his face.

Where the fuck is Fat Mama? he thought.

James couldn’t hold it in. He dropped to his knees and screamed like a bitch giving birth. But he needed to save those tears; he had more to spill. He held his brother’s body in his arms and leaned his forehead against Cain's. He'd never forget this street: Haskell. It was Big T's stomping grounds.

The whole city knew about Big T's son getting kidnapped and the rumors surrounding the brothers, so Hideous had simply fed them to the wolves. He'd made them think they were meeting Salt and Pepper, when the whole time they were heading to their own slaughter.

"Where is Fat Mama?" Judah growled, stepping back outside. He looked down the block and noticed three black Tahoes rolling his way. He tried to run back inside, but it was too late. Gunfire roared through South Dallas.

While the last two members of Fat Mama's family were getting cut like a deck of cards, Hideous was walking through a notorious strip club with a fortune in rare diamonds in his Goyard bag. He passed the strippers shaking ass, never losing sight of the mission. He had one more loose end to tie before he went hunting for Uzi Mi in a foreign city.

Pandora's was just one of many spots he could've met Suwoo Chan, but he chose it for a reason: Salt and Pepper worked there.

He walked toward Suwoo Chan's table. He was surprised the man had even reached out this fast; he thought it would take longer to spark his interest. As he got closer, a large man in a suit stood and glared—a front to make his boss feel safe.

"It's okay," Suwoo said. "He's here to see me. This is an old friend's son."

Hideous took a seat and got straight to business, pouring the diamonds onto the table. The rocks drew the eyes of every man there. Suwoo Chan admired his spirit, even if he didn't love the strategy of selling to the world's elite in a titty bar. Hideous's head was throbbing, but he kept his composure despite the humongous asses walking by.

"This is what I have," Hideous said. Just then, Salt and Pepper hit the stage. They acted a fool, sliding up and down the brass, doing trick after trick. They grabbed Suwoo Chan's attention immediately.

A heavyset Chinese man with a white beard and a ponytail examined the diamonds. He whispered into Suwoo Chan's ear, and Suwoo nodded. He gave his undivided attention to Hideous. "I'll give you $1.7 million for the lot."

Hideous saw a lifetime of freedom when he heard that number. He looked at Suwoo Chan with a wide smile plastered across his face, trying not to sweat. They shook hands, and a FedEx package, thick as a muthafucka, was placed on the table. Inside sat nothing but big faces.

Hideous stood up and said something in Chinese before switching back. "Them strippers on stage? They're my sisters. The daughters of Jephthah Cash."

Suwoo Chan looked up and saw the cold glint of a chrome Snub-nose .38 in Salt's hand. She leveled the snubbie at his chest as Hideous walked calmly away, his back to the pending carnage. The bodyguards were too busy watching the twins' hips to notice the steel until the first shot cracked the air.

With over a million in cash and every ghost from his past deleted, Hideous was finally clear. He checked the weight of the FedEx package in his grip, his eyes already fixed on the horizon. It was time to head to Miami and hunt down Uzi Mi.

To be continued…

Hideous 3

Coming soon

Lock Down Publications and Ca$h Presents Assisted Publishing Packages

Due to an increase in the price of services we have increased our prices. The prices below reflect the price increase as of 11/1/24.

BASIC PACKAGE **$699** Editing Cover Design Formatting	**UPGRADED PACKAGE** **$1000** Typing Editing Cover Design Formatting Upload eBooks to Amazon Upload Paperback to Amazon
ADVANCE PACKAGE **$1,400** Typing Editing (line editing/content) Cover Design Formatting Copyright Registration Proofreading Upload eBooks to Amazon Upload Paperback to Amazon	**LDP SUPREME PACKAGE** **$1,700** Typing Editing (line editing/content) Cover Design Formatting Copyright Registration Proofreading Set up Amazon Account Upload eBooks to Amazon Upload Paperback to Amazon Advertise on LDP's Amazon and Facebook Page

***

Other services available upon request.
Additional charges may apply

Lock Down Publications
P.O. Box 944
Stockbridge, GA 30281-9998
Phone: 470 303-9761
Email: lockdownpublications@gmail.com

Submission Guideline

Submit the first three chapters of your completed manuscript to ldpsubmissions@gmail.com. In the subject line add **Your Book's Title**. The manuscript must be in a Word Doc file and sent as an attachment. Document should be in Times New Roman, double spaced, and in size 12 font. Also, provide your synopsis and full contact information. If sending multiple submissions, they must each be in a separate email.

Have a story but no way to send it electronically? You can still submit to LDP/Ca$h Presents. Send in the first three chapters, written or typed, of your completed manuscript to:

LDP: Submissions Dept
P.O. Box 944
Stockbridge, GA 30281-9998

DO NOT send original manuscript. Must be a duplicate. Provide your synopsis and a cover letter containing your full contact information.

Thanks for considering LDP and Ca$h Presents.

NEW RELEASES

BLOODLINE OF A SAVAGE 1-3

THESE VICIOUS STREETS 1-3

RELENTLESS GOON 1-3

SOULLESS GOON 1&2

BY PRINCE A. TAUHID

THE BUTTERFLY MAFIA 3

BY FUMIYA PAYNE

A THUG'S STREET PRINCESS 1&2

BY MEESHA

CITY OF SMOKE 1-3

BY MOLOTTI

GET IT IN SLUGS 1 &2

BY B. STALL

STANDING ON HER BUSINESS 1&2

BY DG SANTANA

STEPPERS 1,2&3

THE REAL BADDIES OF CHI-RAQ 1-3

BY KING RIO

THE LANE 1-3

BY KEN-KEN SPENCE

THUG OF SPADES 1&2

LOVE IN THE TRENCHES 1&2

CORNER BOYS 1&2

ONCE YOU GO GANGSTA

PROTÉGÉ OF A LEGEND 1- 3

BY COREY ROBINSON

TIL DEATH 3

BY ARYANNA

THE BIRTH OF A GANGSTER 4

BY DELMONT PLAYER

PRODUCT OF THE STREETS 1-3

BY DEMOND "MONEY" ANDERSON

HIDEOUS 2 | TOMMY COOK

MONEY HUNGRY DEMONS 1-2

BY TRANAY ADAMS

TRAP STARS

BY B. SHELLY

HUB CITY MENACE 1-4

BY J. WHITE

A THUGGISH PASSION 1&2

LAND OF DA HOOLIGANZ 1-4

KILLAZ ON STANDBY 1&2

FRESH OFF DA PORCH 1-3

SECURE DA BAG

AMBITIONS OF A SLIDER

FOR MY ENEMIES SAKE

SOULLESS GOON 1&2

FO'EVA ROLLIN 1-4

BY ASSA RAYMOND BAKER

THE LEVEL UP 1&2

BY LUXURY KING

HUNGRY FOR MONEY 1&2

SLIMBOS

QUEEN OF NAPTOWN 1&2

THA TAKEOVER 1-3

BY KEITH CHANDLER

DRILL CITY 1&2

BY ZAY'TOWVEN

LOVE ME OR LET ME GO

BY R. FACEY

SAVAGE DREAMZ

BY KING DAVID

MONEY AND DEAD HOMIES

BY DERRICK SUMMERS

A THUGS STREET PRINCESS 3 Coming Soon

BY MEESHA

BETRAYAL OF A G 2

BY RAY VINCI

SAVAGE FAMILY EMPIRE 1&2

SOULLESS GOON 1&2

THE DIRTY SIDE OF MONEY 1,2&3

BY PRINCE

BY THE TRUCKLOAD 1&2

TIPPIN' THE SCALES 1-4

BAD BITCHES WIT GUNZ 1-3

PROBLEM SOLVED 1-3

THE GIRLRILLA AND HER N*GGA

THE SINGLE LADIES

DYIN' TO GET RICH

THE GIRLRILLA AND HER N*GGA

BY CHRISTOPHER "DIESEL" HORNEZES

AVAILABLE NOW

RESTRAINING ORDER 1 & 2

BY CA$H & COFFEE

LOVE KNOWS NO BOUNDARIES 1-3

BY COFFEE

RAISED AS A GOON I, II, III & IV

BRED BY THE SLUMS I, II, III

BLAST FOR ME I & II

ROTTEN TO THE CORE I II III

A BRONX TALE I, II, III

DUFFLE BAG CARTEL I II III IV V VI

HEARTLESS GOON I II III IV V

A SAVAGE DOPEBOY I II

DRUG LORDS I II III

CUTTHROAT MAFIA I II

KING OF THE TRENCHES

BY GHOST

PUSH IT TO THE LIMIT

BY BRE' HAYES

LAY IT DOWN I & II

LAST OF A DYING BREED I II

BLOOD STAINS OF A SHOTTA I & II III

BY JAMAICA

LOYAL TO THE GAME I II III

LIFE OF SIN I, II III

BY TJ & JELISSA

IF LOVING HIM IS WRONG…I & II

LOVE ME EVEN WHEN IT HURTS I II III

BY JELISSA

BLOODY COMMAS I & II

SKI MASK CARTEL I, II & III

KING OF NEW YORK I II, III IV V

RISE TO POWER I II III

COKE KINGS I II III IV V

BORN HEARTLESS I II III IV

KING OF THE TRAP I II

BY T.J. EDWARDS

WHEN THE STREETS CLAP BACK I & II III

THE HEART OF A SAVAGE I II III IV

MONEY MAFIA I II

LOYAL TO THE SOIL I II III

BY JIBRIL WILLIAMS

A DISTINGUISHED THUG STOLE MY HEART I II & III

LOVE SHOULDN'T HURT I II III IV

RENEGADE BOYS 1-4

PAID IN KARMA 1-3

SAVAGE STORMS 1-3

AN UNFORESEEN LOVE 1-3

BABY, I'M WINTERTIME COLD 1-3

A THUG'S STREET PRINCESS 1,2&3

EMBRACING THE LOVE OF A BOSS 1&2

BY MEESHA

CUM FOR ME 1-8

AN LDP EROTICA COLLABORATION

WHEN A GOOD GIRL GOES BAD

BY ADRIENNE

A GANGSTER'S CODE 1-3

A GANGSTER'S SYN 1-3

THE SAVAGE LIFE 1-3

CHAINED TO THE STREETS 1-3

BLOOD ON THE MONEY 1-3

A GANGSTA'S PAIN 1-3

BEAUTIFUL LIES AND UGLY TRUTHS

CHURCH IN THESE STREETS

BY J-BLUNT

BLOOD OF A BOSS 1-5

SHADOWS OF THE GAME

TRAP BASTARD

BY ASKARI

THE STREETS BLEED MURDER 1-3

THE HEART OF A GANGSTA 1-3

BY JERRY JACKSON

THE COST OF LOYALTY 1-3

BY KWELI

BRIDE OF A HUSTLA 1-3

THE FETTI GIRLS 1-3

CORRUPTED BY A GANGSTA 1-4

BLINDED BY HIS LOVE

THE PRICE YOU PAY FOR LOVE 1-3

DOPE GIRL MAGIC 1-3

BY DESTINY SKAI

A KINGPIN'S AMBITION

A KINGPIN'S AMBITION II

I MURDER FOR THE DOUGH

BY AMBITIOUS

WHITE BOYS 1&2

BY BANDEMIC

A DOPEBOY'S PRAYER

BY EDDIE "WOLF" LEE

I RIDE FOR MY HITTA

I STILL RIDE FOR MY HITTA

BY MISTY HOLT

TRUE SAVAGE 1-7

DOPE BOY MAGIC 1-3

MIDNIGHT CARTEL 1-3

CITY OF KINGZ 1&2

NIGHTMARE ON SILENT AVE

THE PLUG OF LIL MEXICO 1&2

CLASSIC CITY

BY CHRIS GREEN

BACK IN BLOOD 1&2

SEX, MURDER AND GOD 1&2

COUNTDOWN OF A KILLA 1&2

GUNS DOWN, BOTTOMS UP 1&2

DEATH OF A SIDE CHICK

BY LO-LIFE

THE KING CARTEL 1-3

BY FRANK GRESHAM

THESE NIGGAS AIN'T LOYAL 1-3

BY NIKKI TEE

A GANGSTER'S REVENGE 1-4

THE BOSS MAN'S DAUGHTERS 1-5

A SAVAGE LOVE 1&2

BAE BELONGS TO ME 1&2

A HUSTLER'S DECEIT 1-3

WHAT BAD BITCHES DO 1-3

SOUL OF A MONSTER 1-3

KILL ZONE

A DOPE BOY'S QUEEN 1-3

TIL DEATH 1-3

IMMA DIE BOUT MINE 1-6

DYING FOR LIKES 1&2

KILLA CREW 1&2

BY ARYANNA

GANGSTA SHYT 1-3

BY CATO

THE ULTIMATE BETRAYAL

BY PHOENIX

BOSS'N UP 1-3

BY ROYAL NICOLE

I LOVE YOU TO DEATH

BY DESTINY J

LOVE & CHASIN' PAPER

BY QAY CROCKETT

TO DIE IN VAIN

SINS OF A HUSTLA

BY ASAD

BROOKLYN HUSTLAZ

BY BOOGSY MORINA

BROOKLYN ON LOCK 1 & 2

BY SONOVIA

GANGSTA CITY

BY TEDDY DUKE

THE STREETS ARE CALLING

BY DUQUIE WILSON

A DRUG KING AND HIS DIAMOND 1-3

A DOPEMAN'S RICHES

HER MAN, MINE'S TOO 1&2

CASH MONEY HO'S

THE WIFEY I USED TO BE 1&2

PRETTY GIRLS DO NASTY THINGS

BY NICOLE GOOSBY

LIPSTICK KILLAH 1-3

CRIME OF PASSION 1-3

FRIEND OR FOE 1-3

BY MIMI

TRAPHOUSE KING 1-3

KINGPIN KILLAZ 1-3

STREET KINGS 1&2

PAID IN BLOOD 1&2

CARTEL KILLAZ 1-3

DOPE GODS 1&2

BY HOOD RICH

MARRIED TO A BOSS 1-3

BY DESTINY SKAI & CHRIS GREEN

STEADY MOBBN' 1-3

THE STREETS STAINED MY SOUL 1-3

BY MARCELLUS ALLEN

WHO SHOT YA 1-3

SON OF A DOPE FIEND 1-4

HEAVEN GOT A GHETTO 1&2

SKI MASK MONEY 1&2

BY RENTA

FUK SHYT

BY BLAKK DIAMOND

GORILLAZ IN THE BAY 1-4

TEARS OF A GANGSTA 1/&2

3X KRAZY 1&2

STRAIGHT BEAST MODE 1&2

BY DE'KARI

TRIGGADALE 1-3

MURDA WAS THE CASE 1-3

BY ELIJAH R. FREEMAN

SLAUGHTER GANG 1-3

RUTHLESS HEART 1-3

BY WILLIE SLAUGHTER

KINGZ OF THE GAME 1-7

CRIME BOSS 1-4

BY PLAYA RAY

DON'T F#CK WITH MY HEART 1&2

BY LINNEA

GOD BLESS THE TRAPPERS 1-3

THESE SCANDALOUS STREETS 1-3

FEAR MY GANGSTA 1-5

THESE STREETS DON'T LOVE NOBODY 1-2

BURY ME A G 1-5

A GANGSTA'S EMPIRE 1-4

THE DOPEMAN'S BODYGAURD 1&2

THE REALEST KILLAZ 1-3

THE LAST OF THE OGS 1-3

BY TRANAY ADAMS

ADDICTED TO THE DRAMA 1-3

IN THE ARM OF HIS BOSS

BY JAMILA

LOYALTY AIN'T PROMISED 1&2

BY KEITH WILLIAMS

YAYO 1-4

A SHOOTER'S AMBITION 1&2

BRED IN THE GAME

BY S. ALLEN

TRAP GOD 1-3

RICH $AVAGE 1-3

MONEY IN THE GRAVE 1-3

CARTEL MONEY 1&2

BY MARTELL TROUBLESOME BOLDEN

FOREVER GANGSTA 1&2

GLOCKS ON SATIN SHEETS 1&2

BY ADRIAN DULAN

TOE TAGZ 1-4

LEVELS TO THIS SHYT 1&2

IT'S JUST ME AND YOU

BY AH'MILLION

KINGPIN DREAMS 1-3

RAN OFF ON DA PLUG

BY PAPER BOI RARI

THE STREETS MADE ME 1-3

BY LARRY D. WRIGHT

CONFESSIONS OF A GANGSTA 1-4

CONFESSIONS OF A JACKBOY 1-3

CONFESSIONS OF A HITMAN

CONFESSIONS OF A DOPE BOY

BY NICHOLAS LOCK

CAUGHT UP IN THE LIFE 1-3

THE STREETS NEVER LET GO 1-3

BY ROBERT BAPTISTE

HIDEOUS 2 | TOMMY COOK

I'M NOTHING WITHOUT HIS LOVE

SINS OF A THUG

TO THE THUG I LOVED BEFORE

A GANGSTA SAVED XMAS

IN A HUSTLER I TRUST

BY MONET DRAGUN

QUIET MONEY 1-3

THUG LIFE 1-3

EXTENDED CLIP 1&2

A GANGSTA'S PARADISE

BY TRAI'QUAN

THE STREETS WILL NEVER CLOSE 1-3

BY K'AJJI

NEW TO THE GAME 1-3

MONEY, MURDER & MEMORIES 1-3

BY MALIK D. RICE

CREAM 2-3

THE STREETS WILL TALK

BY YOLANDA MOORE

THE ULTIMATE SACRIFICE 1-6

KHADIFI

IF YOU CROSS ME ONCE 1-3

ANGEL 1-4

IN THE BLINK OF AN EYE

BY ANTHONY FIELDS

THE LIFE OF A HOOD STAR

BY CA$H & RASHIA WILSON

CONCRETE KILLA 1-3

VICIOUS LOYALTY 1-3

BLOODY MONEY BAGS 1&2

BY KINGPEN

NIGHTMARES OF A HUSTLA 1-3

BLOOD AND GAMES 1&2

BY KING DREAM

KILLA KOUNTY 1-5

TENDER 1&2

TREACHEROUS YN

BY KHUFU

LIFE OF A SAVAGE 1-4

A GANGSTA'S QUR'AN 1-4

MURDA SEASON 1-3

GANGLAND CARTEL 1-3

CHI'RAQ GANGSTAS 1-4

KILLERS ON ELM STREET 1-3

JACK BOYZ N DA BRONX 1-3

A DOPEBOY'S DREAM 1-3

JACK BOYS VS DOPE BOYS 1-3

COKE GIRLZ

COKE BOYS

SOSA GANG 1&2

BRONX SAVAGES

BODYMORE KINGPINS

BLOOD OF A GOON

BY ROMELL TUKES

HARD AND RUTHLESS 1&2

MOB TOWN 251

THE BILLIONAIRE BENTLEYS 1-3

REAL G'S MOVE IN SILENCE

BY VON DIESEL

HIDEOUS 2 | TOMMY COOK

MOB TIES 1-7

SOUL OF A HUSTLER, HEART OF A KILLER 1-3

GORILLAZ IN THE TRENCHES

OPPS CRY TOO 1-3

THE DAUGHTER OF A CARTEL BOSS 1&2

BY SAYNOMORE

BODYMORE MURDERLAND 1-3

THE BIRTH OF A GANGSTER 1-4

TOP OF THE TRENCHES

BY DELMONT PLAYER

MOBBED UP 1-4

THE BRICK MAN 1-5

THE COCAINE PRINCESS 1-10

STEPPERS 1-3

SUPER GREMLIN 1-5

A GANGSTA'S SON

THE CONNECT'S SECRET

BY KING RIO

MONEY GAME 1&2

BY SMOOVE DOLLA

HIDEOUS 2 | TOMMY COOK

FOR THE LOVE OF A BOSS 1&2

BY C. D. BLUE

LOVE ME OR LET ME GO 1&2

BY R. FACEY

A GANGSTA'S KARMA 1-5

BY FLAME

BLOOD AND MAYHEM

BY JJ DORSEY

KING OF THE TRENCHES 1-3

By GHOST & TRANAY ADAMS

QUEEN OF THE ZOO 1&2

BY BLACK MIGO

GRIMEY WAYS 1-3

BETRAYAL OF A G

BY RAY VINCI

XMAS WITH AN ATL SHOOTER

BY CA$H & DESTINY SKAI

KING KILLA 1&2

PAPER, ROCK, SNAKES

BY VINCENT "VITTO" HOLLOWAY

BETRAYAL OF A THUG 1&2

BY FRE$H

COUNTDOWN OF A KILLA 1&2

SEX, MURDER AND GOD 1&2

GUNS DOWN, BOTTOMS UP 1&2

BY LO-LIFE

FOR THE LOVE OF BLOOD 1-4

BY JAMEL MITCHELL

HOOD CONSIGLIERE 1-3

NO TIME FOR ERROR 1&2

REAL

BY KEESE

THE PLUG'S RUTHLESS DAUGHTER 1,2&3

REDEMPTION IN THE STREETS

BY TONY DANIELS

MOAN IN MY MOUTH

BY XTASY

BORN IN THE GRAVE 1-3

CRIME PAYS 1-3

By Self Made Tay

TORN BETWEEN A GANGSTER AND A GENTLEMAN

BY J-BLUNT

LOYALTY IS EVERYTHING 1-3

CITY OF SMOKE 1-3

BY MOLOTTI

HERE TODAY GONE TOMORROW 1&2

BY FLY ROCK

WOMEN LIE MEN LIE 1-4

FIFTY SHADES OF SNOW 1-3

STACK BEFORE YOU SPLURGE

GIRLS FALL LIKE DOMINOES

NAÏVE TO THE STREETS

BY ROY MILLIGAN

PILLOW PRINCESS

BY S. HAWKINS

THE BUTTERFLY MAFIA 1-3

SALUTE MY SAVAGERY 1&2

BY FUMIYA PAYNE

THE LANE 1&2

BY KEN-KEN SPENCE

THE PUSSY TRAP 1-5

BY NENE CAPRI

DIRTY DNA

BY BLAQUE

SANCTIFIED AND HORNY

BY XTASY

THE RUTHLESS LIFE

HIDEOUS

BY TOMMY COOK

BOOKS BY LDP'S CEO, CA$H

TRUST IN NO MAN

TRUST IN NO MAN 2

TRUST IN NO MAN 3

BONDED BY BLOOD

SHORTY GOT A THUG

THUGS CRY

THUGS CRY 2

THUGS CRY 3

TRUST NO BITCH

TRUST NO BITCH 2

TRUST NO BITCH 3

TIL MY CASKET DROPS

RESTRAINING ORDER

RESTRAINING ORDER 2

IN LOVE WITH A CONVICT

LIFE OF A HOOD STAR

XMAS WITH AN ATL SHOOTER

www.ingramcontent.com/pod-product-compliance
Lightning Source LLC
LaVergne TN
LVHW020717110826
845149LV00012B/2302